Ovid

P. Ovidii Nasonis Heroides, epist, V., XIII

with introduction and notes

Ovid

P. Ovidii Nasonis Heroides, epist, V., XIII
with introduction and notes

ISBN/EAN: 9783337195311

Printed in Europe, USA, Canada, Australia, Japan

Cover: Foto ©Andreas Hilbeck / pixelio.de

More available books at **www.hansebooks.com**

Canadian Collegiate Classics.

P. OVIDII NASONIS HEROIDES.

EPIST. V. XIII.

WITH INTRODUCTION AND NOTES.

TORONTO :

WILLING & WILLIAMSON.

1880.

CONTENTS.

INTRODUCTION.

LIFE AND WORKS OF OVID.

Publius Ovidius Naso was born on the 20th of March (the second day of the ' Quinquatria'), 43 B.C., the year in which the battles fought against Antony under the walls of Modena proved fatal to Hirtius and Pansa, in which the second triumvirate was formed, and in which Cicero perished. The place of his nativity was Sulmo (Sulmone), a town in the cold moist hills of the Peligni, one of the Sabine clans, situated at a short distance to the S. E. of Corfinium, about ninety miles from Rome. His father was of an ancient equestrian family, and Publius was the second son, his elder brother being exactly twelve months his senior. They were both brought up at Rome, their education was superintended by the most distinguished masters, and at the usual period each assumed the manly gown. The elder, a youth of great promise, devoted himself with zeal to the study of eloquence, but his career was short, for he died in his twenty-first year.

Publius repaired to Athens for the purpose of finishing his studies ; at this or some subsequent period he visited, in the train of Macer, the gorgeous cities of Asia, and on his return home passed nearly a year in Sicily. From a very early period he had displayed a decided taste for poetical composition. He soon manifested a rooted aversion to the jarring contentions of the forum, and, notwithstanding the remonstrances of his father, gradually abandoned public life, and devoted himself exclusively to the cultivation of the muses. When a very young man he exercised the functions of triumvir, decemvir, centumvir, and judicial arbiter, but never attempted to rise to any of the higher offices of state, which would have entitled him to the rank and privileges of a senator.

He was married three times. His first wife, whom he wedded while still almost a boy, he describes as unworthy of his affection; his second was of blameless character, but from her also he was soon divorced. One of these two ladies, we know not which, belonged to the Etrurian tribe, whose chief town was Falerii (Santa Maria di Faleri). His third wife was of the noble Fabian family. To her he was deeply attached, and she remained fond and true to the last, supporting him by her faithful affection during the misfortunes which darkened the close of his life.

For a long period fortune had smiled steadily upon Ovid. He was now upwards of fifty years old; the greater part of this time he had spent at Rome, in ease, tranquillity, and happiness. His time was completely at his own disposal, and he could devote what portion of it he pleased to his favourite pursuits; his works were universally popular; he was the companion and friend of all the great political and literary characters of that brilliant epoch; he enjoyed the favour and patronage of the Emperor himself. But he was not destined to end his days in peace. Towards the end of A.D. 8 an order was suddenly conveyed to him from Augustus, commanding that he should instantly quit the metropolis, and fix his residence at Tomi, a colony planted among the Getae, in the midst of barbarous and hostile tribes, on the bleak shores of the Euxine, near the mouth of the Danube. To hear was to obey. Paralysed by grief, he tore himself from the arms of his afflicted wife, and set forth in the dead of winter for the place of his destination which he reached the following spring.

The cause of this banishment is a problem which has excited the curiosity and exercised the ingenuity of learned men ever since the revival of letters, but it is one which our present sources of knowledge do not enable us to solve. The ostensible reason was the immoral tendency of the Ars Amatoria, but the most probable is that he had become accidentally acquainted with some of the intrigues of Julia, the profligate granddaughter of the Emperor, whose well-known sensibility in all matters affecting the honour of his family rendered him unable to tolerate the presence of a man who had been an eye-witness to the infamy of one of its members.

Ninety-six poems in Elegiac verse serve as a sad chronicle of the sufferings he endured during his journey, and while in exile. They exhibit a melancholy picture of the mental prostration of the gay, witty, voluptuous Roman, suddenly snatched from the midst of the most polished society of the age, from the exciting pleasures of the capital of the world, from the charms of a delicious climate, and abandoned to his own resources among a horde of rude soldier peasants, in a remote half-civilized frontier garrison, beneath a Scythian sky. Notwithstanding the exertions of many and powerful friends ; notwithstanding the expostulations, entreaties, prayers, and servile abasement of the unfortunate victim, Augustus and his successor Tiberius remained alike inexorable, and Ovid died of a broken heart in the sixtieth year of his age, and in the tenth of his banishment.

The following list contains all the works usually attributed to Ovid now extant, arranged in the order in which they were composed, in so far as this can be ascertained. Doubts have been entertained with regard to the three last of the series, numbered IX., X., XI., but they are generally received as authentic :—

I. Heroides. A collection of twenty-one letters in Elegiac verse, feigned to have been written by ladies or chiefs in the Heroic age to the absent objects of their love. Doubts have been entertained by some critics, but without good reason, of the genuineness of the last six of these ; others confine their suspicions to the seventeenth, nineteenth, and twenty-first ; while a third party object to the fifteenth alone. The pieces rejected are attributed to Aulus Sabinus, a contemporary poet, the author of several epistles in answer to those composed by Ovid, three of which have been preserved, and are frequently appended to complete editions of the works of the latter.

II. Amores, v. Libri Amorum. Forty nine elegies, chiefly upon amatory subjects, originally divided by the poet into five books, but subsequently reduced by himself to three.

III. Ars Amatoria. A didactic poem in Elegiac verse.

IV. Remedia Amoris. A didactic poem in Elegiac verse. It was written 1 B.C. or A.D. 1, for in v. 155 he speaks of the campaigns of Caius Cæsar as actually in progress.

V. Metamorphoseon Libri XV. An extensive collection, in fifteen books, of the most remarkable fables of ancient mythology, which involved a transformation of shape, extending in a continuous series from Chaos down to the death of Julius Cæsar. The metre employed is the Dactylic Hexameter. This work had not received its last polish when its author was driven into exile. In the bitterness of his heart he committed this and several other compositions to the flames, but copies had fortunately been already circulated among his friends, and their destruction was thus prevented.

VI. Fastorum Libri VI. An exposition in Elegiac verse of the numerous festivals in the Roman Calendar, containing a detailed description of the various ceremonies, together with historical and antiquarian investigations regarding their origin. The holy-days are enumerated, in succession, from the beginning of the year, a book being devoted to each month. Of these, six are extant, commencing with January and ending with June. This was one of the compositions which was unfinished at the time of Ovid's banishment; he intended to have carried it on through the whole year, although there is no reason to believe that he ever completed his design.

VII. VIII. Tristium Libri V., Epistolarum ex Ponto Libri IV. The former a collection of fifty elegies, in five books; the latter of forty-six elegies, in four books. The whole of these were produced at Tomi, with the exception of those forming the first book of the Tristia, which appear to have been written on the journey thither. They are entirely occupied with the lamentations of the poet over his sad destiny, a description of the sufferings he endured, and supplications for a remission of his sentence. The

Epistolae ex Ponto are addressed to different individuals, for the most part persons residing at Rome and connected with the Court, who are implored to use their good offices with the Emperor and the different members of the royal family.

IX. Ibis. Six hundred and forty-six lines in Elegiac verse, consisting of a series of maledictions poured forth against an enemy whose name is concealed, written immediately after the banishment of the poet, as we learn from the commencement,

'Tempus ad hoc, lustris iam bis mihi quinque peractis,
Omne fuit Musae carmen inerme meae.'

It is an imitation of a lost poem by Callimachus, directed against Apollonius of Rhodes, and bearing the same title. The origin of the appellation is unknown.

X. Halieuticon Liber. A mutilated fragment, in Hexameter verse, of a Natural History of Fishes. One hundred and thirty-two lines only have been preserved.

XI Medicamina Faciei. Another fragment, in Elegiac verse, of a didactic poem on the composition and use of cosmetics. Of this one hundred lines remain.

Two other pieces are frequently found in MSS. of Ovid, but the best critics are of opinion that both must be attributed to some other author or authors. The first of these, 'Consolatio ad Liviam Augustam,' is a sort of dirge on the Death of Drusus, who perished in Germany, 9 B.C. It is in Elegiac verse, and extends to four hundred and seventy-four lines. The other, also in Elegiac verse, and containing one hundred and eighty-two lines, is entitled 'Nux,' and is a lamentation poured forth by a walnut-tree on account of the indignities offered to it by travellers and passers by, followed up by a declamation against the avarice and profligacy of the age in general.

Ovid in early life cultivated dramatic literature, and, it would seem, with marked success, for his tragedy 'Medea' is highly extolled by Quinctilian.

The metre in which the Heroïdes is composed is the so-called Elegīac couplet, that is, a Hexameter, or ordinary Heroic line (like that of Virgil's Æneid), followed by a Dactylic Pentameter, which was hardly ever used but in connection with the Hexameter. The following is a scheme of the present way of scanning the Elegiac couplet:

(1)   – ◡◡ | – ◡◡ | – ◡◡ | – ◡◡ | – ◡◡ | – –

(2)   – ◡◡ | – ◡◡ | – ‖ – ◡◡ | – ◡◡ | ⏒

An older way of scanning the Pentameter was:

– ◡◡ | – ◡◡ | – – | ◡◡ – | ◡◡ – |

that is, with a Spondee in the middle followed by two Anapæsts.

1. The Hexameter consists of six feet, of which the fifth is a Dactyl, the sixth a Spondee, while the first four may be Dactyls or Spondees. Licenses of any kind are but sparingly admitted in the Hexameter of this couplet.

2. The Dactylic Pentameter, as usually scanned, consists of two members separated by the Penthemimeral pause. The first member has two feet—Dactyls or Spondees—followed by a long syllable ; the second member is made up of two Dactyls followed by a syllable, which, whether long or short, is considered long.

Ovid, who presents the best models of Elegīac verse, usually observes the following, among other rules :

(a) If the sense overflow the limits of the Hexameter, and be completed in the first word of the Pentameter, then the first foot of this latter should be a Dactyl.

(b) Elisions should be sparingly employed.

(c) Each couplet should make sense by itself.

(*d*) The Pentameter should end in a dissyllable, which should be some emphatic part of speech.

(*e*) The last syllable, if short, should end in a consonant.

(*f*) If the last syllable of the *first* member of the Pentameter be a monosyllable (which should rarely happen), another long monosyllable should precede, or a dissyllable of two short syllables. An exception to this is admitted in the case of the monosyllable *est*, when the preceding vowel is elided.

EXAMPLES OF THE SCANNING OF THE ELEGIAC COUPLET.

Quīs tĭbĭ | mōnstrā- | bāt sal- | tus vē- | nātĭbŭs | āptōs,
   Et tĕgĕ- | rēt cătŭ- | lōs‖quā fĕră | rūpĕ sŭ- | ōs ?
Rētĭă | sāepĕ cŏ- | mēs măcŭ- | lis dīs- | tīnctă tĕ- | tēndĭ ;
   Sāepĕ cĭ- | tōs ē- | gī ‖ pĕr jŭgă | sūmmă că- | nes.

P. OVIDII NASONIS
HEROIDES.

EPIST. V.—OENONE PARIDI.

Perlegis? an conjux prohibet nova? perlege! non est
  Ista Mycenaea litera facta manu.
Pegasis Oenone, Phrygiis celeberrima silvis,
  Laesa queror de te, si sinis ipse, meo.
Quis deus opposuit nostris sua numina votis?   5
  Ne tua permaneam, quod mihi crimen obest?
Leniter, ex merito quicquid patiare, ferendum est.
  Quae venit indigne poena, dolenda venit.
Nondum tantus eras, cum te contenta marito,
  Edita de magno flumine nympha fui.   10
Qui nunc Priamides, absit reverentia vero,
  Servus eras; servo nubere nympha tuli.
Saepe greges inter requievimus arbore tecti,
  Mixtaque cum foliis praebuit herba torum.
Saepe super stramen fenoque jacentibus alto   15
  Defensa est humili cana pruina casa.
Quis tibi monstrabat saltus venatibus aptos,
  Et tegeret catulos qua fera rupe suos?
Retia saepe comes maculis distincta tetendi:
  Saepe citos egi per juga longa canes.   20
Incisae servant a te mea nomina fagi,
  Et legor Oenone falce notata tua:

Et quantum trunci, tantum mea nomina crescunt:
    Crescite, et in titulos surgite recta meos.
Populus est, memini, fluviali consita ripa   25
    Est in qua nostri litera scripta memor.
Popule, vive, precor, quae consita margine ripae
, Hoc in rugoso cortice carmen habes:
' Cum Paris Oenone poterit spirare relicta,
    Ad fontem Xanthi versa recurret aqua.'   30
Xanthe, retro propera, versaeque recurrite lymphae !
    Sustinet Oenonen deseruisse Paris.
Illa dies fatum miserae mihi dixit, ab illa
    Pessima mutati coepit amoris hiems,
Qua Venus et Juno, sumptisque decentior armis   35
    Venit in arbitrium nuda Minerva tuum.
Attoniti micuere sinus, gelidusque cucurrit,
    Ut mihi narrasti, dura per ossa tremor.
Consului, neque enim modice terrebar, anusque
    Longaevosque senes: constitit esse nefas.   40
Caesa abies, sectaeque trabes, et classe parata,
    Caerula ceratas accipit unda rates.
Flesti discedens: hoc saltim parce negare:
    Praeterito magis est iste pudendus amor.
Et flesti, et nostros vidisti flentis ocellos: 45
    Miscuimus lacrimas maestus uterque suas.
Non sic appositis vincitur vitibus ulmus,
    Ut tua sunt collo brachia nexa meo.
Ah ! quotiens, cum te vento quererere teneri,
    Riserunt comites: ille secundus erat.   50
Oscula dimissae quotiens repetita dedisti !
    Quam vix sustinuit dicere lingua ' vale !'

Aura levis rigido pendentia lintea malo
    Suscitat, et remis eruta canet aqua.
Prosequor infelix oculis abeuntia vela,   55
    Qua licet, et lacrimis humet arena meis.
Utque celer venias, virides Nereïdas oro:
    Scilicet ut venias in mea damna celer.
Votis ergo meis alii rediture redisti ?
    Hei mihi, pro dira pellice blanda fui !   60
Aspicit immensum moles nativa profundum:
    Mons fuit: aequoreis illa resistit aquis:
Hinc ego vela tuae cognovi prima carinae,
    Et mihi per fluctus impetus ire fuit.
Dum moror, in summa fulsit mihi purpura prora.   65
    Pertimui ; cultus non erat ille tuus.
Fit propior, terrasque cita ratis attigit aura:
    Femineas vidi corde tremente genas.
Non satis id fuerat ; quid enim furiosa morabar ?
    Haerebat gremio turpis amica tuo.   70
Tunc vero rupique sinus et pectora planxi,
    Et secui madidas ungue rigente genas,
Implevique sacram querulis ululatibus Iden.
    Illuc has lacrimas in mea saxa tuli.
Sic Helene doleat, desertaque conjuge ploret,   75
    Quaeque prior nobis intulit, ipsa ferat.
Nunc tibi conveniunt quae te per aperta sequantur
    Aequora, legitimos destituantque viros.
At cum pauper eras armentaque pastor agebas,
    Nulla nisi Oenone pauperis uxor erat.   80
Non ego miror opes, nec me tua regia tangit,
    Nec de tot Priami dicar ut una nurus.

Non tamen ut Priamus nymphae socer esse recuset,
  Aut Hecubae fuerim dissimulanda nurus.
Dignaque sum et cupio fieri matrona potentis: 85
  Sunt mihi, quas possint sceptra decere, manus.
Nec me, faginea quod tecum fronde jacebam,
  Despice ; purpureo sum magis apta toro.
Denique tutus amor meus est tibi ; nulla parantur
  Bella, nec ultrices advehit unda rates.   90
Tyndaris infestis fugitiva reposcitur armis:
  Hac venit in thalamos dote superba tuos.
Quae si sit Danais reddenda, vel Hectora fratrem,
  Vel cum Deïphobo Polydamanta roga.
Quid gravis Antenor, Priamus quid suadeat ipse,   95
  Consule, quis aetas longa magistra fuit.
Turpe rudimentum, patriae praeponere raptam.
  Causa pudenda tua est; justa vir arma movet.
Nec tibi, si sapias, fidam promitte Lacaenam,
  Quae sit in amplexus tam cito versa tuos.   100
Ut minor Atrides temerati foedera lecti
  Clamat, et externo laesus amore dolet,
Tu quoque clamabis.   Nulla reparabilis arte
  Laesa pudicitia est ; deperit illa semel.
Ardet amore tui ? sic et Menelaon amavit.   105
  Nunc jacet in viduo credulus ille toro.
Felix Andromache, certo bene nupta marito !
  Uxor ad exemplum fratris habenda fui.
Tu levior foliis, tum cum sine pondere suci
  Mobilibus ventis arida facta volant.   110
Et minus est in te, quam summa pondus arista,
  Quae levis assiduis solibus usta riget.

Hoc tua, nam recolo, quondam germana canebat,
  Sic mihi diffusis vaticinata comis
'Quid facis, Oenone? Quid arenae semina mandas?   115
  Non profecturis littora bubus aras.
Graia juvenca venit, quae te patriamque domumque
  , Perdat ! io prohibe ! Graia juvenca venit !
Dum licet, obscenam ponto demergite puppim !
  Heu, quantum Phrygii sanguinis illa vehit !'   120
Dixerat ; in cursu famulae rapuere furentem.
  At mihi flaventes diriguere comae.
Ah ! nimium miserae vates mihi vera fuisti.
  Possidet, en, saltus Graia iuvenca meos !
Sit facie quamvis insignis, adultera certe est.   125
  Deseruit socios hospite capta deos.
Illam de patria Theseus, nisi nomine fallor,
  Nescio quis Theseus abstulit ante sua.
A juvene et cupido credatur reddita virgo ?
  Unde hoc compererim tam bene, quaeris ? amo.   130
Vim licet appelles, et culpam nomine veles:
  Quae totiens rapta est, praebuit ipsa rapi.
At manet Oenone fallenti casta marito:
  Et poteras falli legibus ipse tuis.
Me Satyri celeres, silvis ego tecta latebam,   135
  Quaesierunt rapido, turba proterva, pede,
Cornigerumque caput pinu praecinctus acuta
  Faunus, in immensis qua tumet Ida jugis.
Me fide conspicuus Trojae munitor amavit.   139
  Admisitque meas ad sua dona manus.   145
Quaecumque herba potens ad opem radixque medendi
  Utilis in toto nascitur orbe, mea est.
                          2

Me miseram, quod amor non est medicabilis herbis !
  Deficior prudens artis ab arte mea.
Ipse repertor opis vaccas pavisse Pheraeas   150
  Fertur, et e nostro saucius igne fuit.
Quod nec graminibus tellus fecunda creandis,
  Nec deus, auxilium tu mihi ferre potes.
Et potes, et merui, dignae miserere puellae !
  Non ego cum Danais arma cruenta fero,   155
Sed tua sum tecumque fui puerilibus annis,
  Et tua, quod superest temporis, esse precor.

EPIST. XIII.—LAODAMIA PROTESILAO.

Mittit, et optat amans, quo mittitur, ire salutem,
    Haemonis Haemonio Laodamia viro.
Aulide te fama est, vento retinente, morari:
    Ah ! me cum fugeres, hic ubi ventus erat ?
Tum freta debuerant vestris obsistere remis.   5
    Illud erat saevis utile tempus aquis.
Oscula plura viro mandataque plura dedissem:
    Et sunt quae volui dicere multa tibi.
Raptus es hinc praeceps, et qui tua vela vocaret,
    Quem cuperent nautae, non ego, ventus erat.   10
Ventus erat nautis aptus, non aptus amanti:
    Solvor ab amplexu, Protesilaë, tuo,
Linguaque mandantis verba imperfecta reliquit:
    Vix illud potui dicere triste *vale.*
Incubuit Boreas, abreptaque vela tetendit: 15
    Jamque meus longe Protesilaüs erat.
Dum potui spectare virum, spectare juvabat:
    Sumque tuos oculos usque secuta meis.
Ut te non poteram, poteram tua vela videre,
    Vela diu vultus detinuere meos.   20
At postquam nec te, nec vela fugacia vidi,
    Et quod spectarem, nil nisi pontus erat,
Lux quoque tecum abiit, tenebrisque exsanguis obortis
    Succiduo dicor procubuisse genu.
Vix socer Iphiclus, vix me grandaevus Acastus,   25
    Vix mater gelida maesta refecit aqua.

Officium fecere pium, sed inutile nobis:
 Indignor miserae non licuisse mori.
Ut rediit animus, pariter rediere dolores.
 Pectora legitimus casta momordit amor.   **30**
Nec mihi pectendos cura est praebere capillos,
 Nec libet aurata corpora veste tegi.
Ut quas pampinea tetigisse Bicorniger hasta
 Creditur; huc illuc, qua furor egit, eo.
Conveniunt matres Phylaceïdes, et mihi clamant: **35**
 ' Indue regales, Laodamia, sinus !'
Scilicet ipsa geram saturatas murice lanas,
 Bella sub Iliacis moenibus ille geret ?
Ipsa comas pectar, galea caput ille premetur:
 Ipsa novas vestes, dura vir arma feret ?   **40**
Qua possum, squalore tuos imitata labores
 Dicar, et haec belli tempora tristis agam.
Dyspari Priamide, damno formose tuorum,
 Tam sis hostis iners, quam malus hospes eras.
Aut te Taenariae faciem culpasse maritae,   **45**
 Aut illi vellem displicuisse tuam.
Tu, qui pro rapta nimium, Menelaë, laboras,
 Hei mihi, quam multis flebilis ultor eris !
Di, precor, a nobis omen removete sinistrum,
· Et sua det reduci vir meus arma Jovi.   **50**
Sed timeo, quotiens subiit miserabile bellum:
 More nivis lacrimae sole madentis eunt.
Ilion et Tenedos Simoïsque et Xanthus et Ide
 Nomina sunt ipso paene timenda sono.
Nec rapere ausurus, nisi se defendere posset, **55**
 Hospes erat. vires noverat ille suas.

Venerat, ut fama est, multo spectabilis auro,
  Quique suo Phrygias corpore ferret opes,
Classe virisque potens, per quae fera bella geruntur,
  Et sequitur regni pars quota quemque sui ?   60
His ego te victam, consors Ledaea gemellis,
  Suspicor ; haec Danais posse nocere puto.
Hectora nescio quem timeo: Paris Hectora dixit
  Ferrea sanguinea bella movere manu.
Hectora, quisquis is est, si sum tibi cara, caveto: 65
  Signatum memori pectore nomen habe.
Hunc ubi vitaris, alios vitare memento,
  Et multos illic Hectoras esse puta:
Et facito ut dicas, quotiens pugnare parabis,
  ‘ Parcere me jussit Laodamia sibi.’   70
Si cadere Argolico fas est sub milite Trojam,
  Te quoque non ullum vulnus habente cadat.
Pugnet et adversos tendat Menelaüs in hostes:
  Ut rapiat Paridi, quam Paris ante sibi.
Irruat ; et causa quem vincit et armis.   75
  Hostibus e mediis nupta petenda viro est.
Causa tua est dispar. Tu tantum vivere pugna,
  Inque pios dominae posse redire sinus.
Parcite, Dardanidae, de tot, precor, hostibus uni,
  Ne meus ex illo corpore sanguis eat.   80
Non est, quem deceat nudo concurrere ferro,
  Saevaque in oppositos pectora ferre viros.
Fortius ille potest multo, quam pugnat, amare.
  Bella gerant alii: Protesilaus amet.
Nunc fateor ; volui revocare, animusque ferebat.   85
  Substitit auspicii lingua timore mali.

Cum foribus velles ad Trojam exire paternis,
   Pes tuus offenso limine signa dedit.
Ut vidi, ingemui, tacitoque in pectore dixi
   'Signa reversuri sint, precor, ista viri !'   90
Haec tibi nunc refero, ne sis animosus in armis.
   Fac meus in ventos hic timor omnis eat.
Sors quoque nescio quem fato designat iniquo,
   Qui primus Danaûm Troada tangat humum.
Infelix, quae prima virum lugebit ademptum !   95
   Di faciant, ne tu strenuus esse velis !
Inter mille rates tua sit millesima puppis,
   Jamque fatigatas ultima verset aquas.
Hoc quoque praemoneo ; de nave novissimus exi:
   Non est, quo properes, terra paterna tibi.   100
Cum venies, remoque move veloque carinam,
   Inque tuo celerem litore siste gradum !
Sive latet Phoebus, seu terris altior exstat,
   Tu mihi luce dolor, tu mihi nocte venis:
Nocte tamen quam luce magis; nox grata puellis. 105
   Quarum suppositus colla lacertus habet.
Aucupor in lecto mendaces caelibe somnos.
   Dum careo veris, gaudia falsa juvant.
Sed tua cur nobis pallens occurrit imago ?
   Cur venit a verbis multa querela tuis ?   110
Excutior somno, simulacraque noctis adoro:
   Nulla caret fumo Thessalis ara meo:
Tura damus, lacrimamque super, qua sparsa relucet,
   Ut solet adfuso surgere flamma mero.
Quando ego, te reducem cupidis amplexa lacertis, 115
   Languida laetitia solvar ab ipsa mea ?

Quando erit, ut lecto mecum bene junctus in uno
  Militiae referas splendida facta tuae ?
Quae mihi dum referes, quamvis audire juvabit,
  Multa tamen rapies oscula, multa dabis.   120
Semper in his apte narrantia verba resistunt:
  Promptior est dulci lingua referre mora.
Sed cum Troja subit, subeunt ventique fretumque,
  Spes bona sollicito victa timore cadit.
Hoc quoque, quod venti prohibent exire carinas,   125
  Me movet ; invitis ire paratis aquis.
Quis velit in patriam, vento prohibente, reverti ?
  A patria pelago vela vetante datis !
Ipse suam non praebet iter Neptunus ad urbem.
  Quo ruitis ? Vestras quisque redite domos !   130
Quo ruitis, Danai ? Ventos audite vetantes !
  Non subiti casus, numinis ista mora est.
Quid petitur tanto nisi turpis adultera bello ?
  Dum licet, Inachiae vertite vela rates !
Sed quid ago ? revoco ? revocaminis omen abesto,   135
  Blandaque compositas aura secundet aquas.
Troasin invideo, quae sic lacrimosa suorum
  Funera conspicient, nec procul hostis erit.
Ipsa suis manibus forti nova nupta marito
  Imponet galeam barbaraque arma dabit.   140
Arma dabit, dumque arma dabit, simul oscula sumet :—
  Hoc genus officii dulce duobus erit—
Producetque virum, dabit et mandata reverti,
  Et dicet ‘ referas ista fac arma Jovi !’
Ille, ferens dominae mandata recentia secum   145
  Pugnabit caute, respicietque domum.

Exuet haec reduci clipeum, galeamque resolvet,
    Excipietque suo corpora lassa sinu.
Nos sumus incertae; nos anxius omnia cogit,
    Quae possunt fieri, facta putare timor.   150
Dum tamen arma geres diverso miles in orbe,
    Quae referat vultus est mihi cera tuos.
Illi blanditias, illi tibi debita verba
    Dicimus, amplexus accipit illa meos.
Crede mihi, plus est, quam quod videatur imago, 155
    Adde sonum cerae, Protesilaus erit.
Hanc specto, teneoque sinu pro conjuge vero.
    Et, tamquam possit verba referre, queror.
Per reditus corpusque tuum, mea numina, juro,
    Perque pares animi conjugiique faces,   160
Perque, quod ut videam canis albere capillis,
    Quod tecum possis ipse referre, caput,
Me tibi venturam comitem, quocumque vocaris,
    Sive... quod heu timeo, sive superstes eris.
Ultima mandato claudetur epistola parvo: 165
    Si tibi cura mei, sit tibi cura tui !

NOTES.

EPIST. V.—OENONE PARIDI.

The loves of Paris and Oenone, and the legend regarding the birth and early history of the former, which form the groundwork of this epistle, were unknown to Homer. What follows is the substance of the tale as narrated by Apollodorus.

Hector was the first-born of Priam and Hecuba. When Hecuba was about to produce a second child, she dreamed that she had given birth to a blazing torch, which kindled a conflagration that spread over the whole city. Priam, having been informed by her of the vision, sent for Aesacus (his son by Arisbe, a former wife), who was skilled in the interpretation of dreams, an art which he had been taught by Merops, his maternal grandfather. Aesacus pronounced that the boy would prove the destruction of his country, and bade them expose the babe. · Priam, as soon as it was born, gave it to one of his herdmen, named Agelaus, to be conveyed to Ida and there abandoned. The infant, left to perish, was nurtured for five days by a she-bear, when Agelaus, finding it thus miraculously preserved, took it up and bore it to his dwelling, where he reared it as his own son, under the name of Paris. The child having grown up to manhood, excelled both in comeliness and valour, and soon received the additional appellation of Alexander, because he withstood and drove away the robbers who attacked the flocks. Not long after he discovered his parents.

While yet a shepherd in the hills, he wedded Oenone, daughter of the river Cebren. This nymph, having learned the art of prophecy from Rhea, warned Alexander not to sail in quest of Helen ; but finding that her remonstrances were unheeded, she then enjoined him, should he be wounded, to come to her for aid, since she alone had power to heal him. After this Paris bore away Helen from Sparta, and being pierced, during the war against Troy, by an arrow shot by Philoctetes from the bow of Hercules, he returned again to Ida to seek Oenone's aid. But she, cherishing resentment, refused to exert her skill. Alexander was borne back to Troy, and there expired. Oenone having repented, brought drugs to heal his wound, and finding him a corpse, hanged herself for grief.

It will be seen that Ovid adheres, for the most part, closely to the above tale, departing from it in one or two points only.

1. In some MSS. this epistle commences with the following couplet, which is generally considered spurious:

Nympha suo Paridi (quamvis meus esse recuses),
Mittit ab Idaeis verba legenda jugis.

Perlegis...manu. 'Dost thou read this through ? or, does thy new wife hinder thee ? Read it through ! This letter is not written by the hand of him of Mycenæ.'

2. **Mycenaea manu,** i.e., hostili, with reference to Agamemnon and Menelaus, sons of Atreus, King of Mycenae.

3. **Pegasis Oenone.** 'Oenone the fountain nymph,' from πηγή a fountain. Oenone was the daughter of the river Cebren. Many ancient writers speak of the 'Cebrenia Regio' and its capital 'Cebrene' in the Troad. The river

Cebren is mentioned, as we have seen above, in the narrative of Apollodorus. Geographers fix the site of 'Cebrene' near the sources of the 'Mendere' (which some identify with the Scamander, and others with the Simois of Homer) in mount Ida. Extensive ruins mark the spot, now called 'Kutchunlu-Tepe,' and a little way above these a small stream, believed to be the 'Cebren,' falls into the 'Mendere,' and is called the 'Kaz-daghtchai.' With regard to the epithet ' Pegasis,' we may observe that the Muses are styled ' Pegasides ' by Propert. 3. 1, 19,

Mollia, Pegasides, vestro date serta poetae.

Si sinis ipse, meo. 'Who art mine, if thou thyself dost permit it.'

6. **Ne tua permaneam.** 'From remaining thine.'

7. **Leniter...ferendum est.** 'Whatever you suffer deservedly should be borne with patience.'

8. **Dolenda.** 'As a ground for complaint.' Lit. 'to be grieved over.'

9. **Tantus,** i.e., nondum agnitus eras Priamifilius. In v. 12, he is termed ' servus,' because he was at that time the reputed son of the bondsman of Priam.

11. Remark the difference of meaning according as we read **adsit** or **absit**.

Absit. ' Ita revereamur veritatem, ut eam quamvis tibi ingrata sit, confiteamur.'

Adsit. 'Ne tui reverentia nos impediat quominus verum dicamus.'

Priamides. 'The son of Priam.'

12. **Tuli,** i.e., non recusavi nubere.

15. **Super stramen fenoque jacentibus.** Remark the change in the construction of 'stramen' and 'feno.'

16. **Defensa.** 'Defendere' signifies properly 'to ward off,' so Virg. E. 7. 47,

> *Solstitium pecori defendite, jam venit aestas,*

and Senec. de Prov. 4,

> *Imbrem culmo aut fronde defendunt.*

19. **Maculis.** The knots of a net seem to be indicated by 'maculae.' N. Heins. would understand the coloured feathers employed to scare the beasts of chase, and drive them into the toils, as in Virg. G. 3. 372.

> *Hos* (sc. *cervos*) *non immissis canibus, non cassibus ullis,*
> *Puniceaeve agitant trepidos formidine pennae.*

Scheller in his Lexicon says the 'maculae' are the 'meshes' or 'holes' of the net. The word cannot bear either of the two last mentioned significations in the following passage from Varro, R. R. 3. 11, where he is giving directions for the construction of a νησσοτροφεῖον or duck-yard. After describing the manner in which the wall is to be built and plastered, he continues—*idque saeptum totum rete grandibus maculis integitur ne eo involare aquila possit, neve ex eo evolare anas ;*—and so Columella, 8. 15, almost in the same words. In these passages 'grandibus maculis' must mean 'strong knots,' for 'large meshes' would admit of the very evil which the farmer is here taught to guard against.

20. **Per juga longa.** 'Over the long mountain ranges.'

22. **Legor...tua.** 'I am read of as thine.'

24. **Recta**, although found in most MSS., is scarcely intelligible, since it cannot be connected either with 'trunci' or ' nomina.' 'Rite,' which appears in two MSS., is probably the true reading. 'Recte' was perhaps placed in the margin as an explanation of 'rite,' and might then find its way into the text, and finally would be changed into 'recta,' to prevent a violation of the laws of prosody.

25. **Consita.** 'Sero' and its compounds are used perpetually by Virgil and the prose writers upon agriculture, in the sense of ' to plant.' as well as in that of ' to sow.'

27. **Popule.** Distinguish between pōpulus and pŏpulus.

Quae hoc ..habes. 'Which...hast these lines inscribed on thy rough bark.'

30. **Ad fontem.** The expression of rivers running backwards seems to have been applied proverbially, among the Greeks, to anything which was so strange as to seem a violation of the laws of nature. So the chorus in the Medea of Euripides, and in like manner Horace, when expressing his astonishment at the resolution of Iccius, Od. I. 29, 10:

> *Quis neget arduis*
> *Pronos relabi posse rivos*
> *Montibus, et Tiberim reverti.*

31. **Lymphae.** ' Et *lympha* et *nympha* pro aqua ponitur; verum ubi poetae aquis actionem quandam humanam tribuunt, *nympham* potius quam *lympham*, dicunt.—Itaque Heins. e MSS. emendat *nymphae*' R.

The two words, as might be expected from their resemblance both in form and meaning, are perpetually confounded in MSS.

32. Sustinet, nearly the same as 'tuli' in v. 12, imply-ing that a person brings himself by an effort to do some-thing from which he would naturally shrink. It occurs again in v. 52.

33. Fatum...dixit. 'Pronounced my doom.'

Ab illa. Sc. *die.*

35. **Qua.** 'On which' day.

37. Micuere sinus. 'Mico' properly signifies ' to move rapidly backwards and forwards;' thus Virgil of a high-bred horse, G. 3. 84,

> *Stare loco, nescit, micat auribus, et tremit artus,*

and of a serpent darting its tongue, G. 3. 439,

> *et linguis micat ore trisulcis.*

It is often applied, as in the present passage, to mental agi-tation, thus *attoniti micuere sinus—corda micant regis— pulsantur trepidi corde micante sinus, &c.,* are all Ovidian expressions.

41. Classe parata, the reading adopted by Burmann [peracta] and approved by Ruhnken, can scarcely be defended. ' Parare' and ' ornare' are the technical words employed by the best writers with regard to the equipment of a fleet, while not a single example can be produced in favour of ' peragere.' In the passages quoted from Suetonius Calig. 21, and Oth. 6, it is applied to buildings the construction of which required great time and toil.

42. Ceratas, i.e. cera piceque oblitas, so again Ov. R. A. 447,

> *Non satis una tenet ceratas ancora puppes.*

43. Parce negare, i.e. noli negare, cave neges.

This use of the verb ' parco ' is very common among the poets, although scarcely admissible in prose composition, e.g. Hor. Od. 3. 8, 26,

> *Parce privatus nimium cavere,*

and Virg. E. 3. 94,

> *Parcite, oves nimium procedere non bene ripae*
> *Creditur.*

44. Praeterito, ' the love which once you bore to me, but which now has passed away.'

45. Nostros vidisti flentis ocellos, i.e. mei flentis ocellos. This peculiar construction, by which the possessive pronoun is substituted for the genitive of the personal, is found occasionally in the best writers.

> *quum mea nemo*
> *Scripta legat vulgo recitare timentis.* Hor. S. I. 4, 22.

The same idiom is found in Greek, Hom. Il. 3. 180.

46. Miscuimus...suas. 'We both in sorrow mingled our tears."

49. Cum te...teneri. ' When thou didst complain of being detained by the wind.'

50. Ille secundus erat. ' Scilicet mihi amanti, quia te retinebat, nec illo flante abire poteras ' B.

A singular misapprehension of the meaning. Oenone intends to say that when the wind was really favourable for the voyage, Paris, unable to tear himself from her arms, and eager to frame an excuse for delay, complained that it was adverse, a pretext so flimsy that 'riserunt comites.'

53. **Rigido malo**. 'From the erect mast.'

54. **Eruta**. 'Translatio ducta est ex agricultura ; nam proprie fossor dicitur *eruere terram*' R. We have a double metaphor in Ov. Amor. 3. 8, 43,

Non freta demissi verrebant eruta remi.

Canet. 'Is white.'

56. **Qua licet**. 'As far as I could.'

57. **Nereidas**. The Nereïdes (Nereïs, Nereïdis) were sea-nymphs, and daughters of Nereus.

58. **Scilicet ut...celer**. 'That, to my misfortune, for-sooth, thou mayest speedily return.'

59. **Alii**, 'est dativus commodi, ut grammatici loquun-tur' R.

Votis ergo meis. This line is probably corrupt, for the final syllable in 'ergo' is uniformly made long by the writers of the Augustan age, and by Ovid himself elsewhere. See the question fully discussed in 'Ramsay's Manual of Latin Prosody,' p. 58.

60. **Pellice**, i.e. Helena.

Blanda, i.e. supplex—precibus delinivi Deas marinas.

61. **Nativa**, i.e. 'the work of nature,' as opposed to any bulwark reared by the hand of man. So in the Fasti, 5. 149,

Est moles nativa : loco res nomina fecit :
Appellant saxum : pars bona montis ea est.

64. **Impetus**, 'impulse,' as opposed to *ratio*, 'a medi-tated plan.'

Et quod nunc ratio est, impetus ante fuit. Ov. R. A. 10.

65. **Purpura.** 'A purple garment.'

66. **Cultus.** 'Apparel.'

69. **Morabar.** 'Haec non intelligo: forte rectius *morabor* cum Leidensi codice' H. The meaning is this:

' It was not enough that I beheld with fluttering heart a woman's cheek—for had that been enough to satisfy me of your infidelity, why did I madly linger? No, I did not believe the worst, until, upon a nearer view, I saw an impure mistress clasped in your embrace—there was no longer any room for doubt—*Tunc vero rupique sinus et pectora planxi,*' &c.

Heusinger and Jahn read

Non satis id fuerat? quid enim furiosa morabar?

but the interrogation of the first member of the clause does not suit the 'quid enim' which follows. Ruhnken, who adopts this punctuation, understands it thus : ' Cur me non subduxi, ut Helenam ne viderem in gremio tuo haerentem.' The explanation of Burmann is harder to understand than the passage itself.

71. **Sinus,** i.e., vestes. Properly speaking, 'the folds of the garment;' it is used in the same general sense in Ep. 13, 36,

Induc regales, Laodamia, sinus.

Rupi. ' I rent.'

73. **Idam** *v.* **Iden.** A number of nouns of the first declension, chiefly proper names, are employed by the poets, sometimes under their Greek, sometimes under their Latin shape, as best suits their purpose. Thus we have ' Ida ' and ' Ide ;' ' Leda,' ' Lede ;' ' Helena,' ' Helene ;' ' Creta,'

'Crete ;' and many others. Where either form is equally admissible, as in the present passage, we must be guided entirely by the best MSS.

Sacram...Iden. 'Sacra dicitur' quod Cybeles sacra in hoc monte celebrabantur, quae inde etiam *matris Idaeae* nomen habet' R.

74. **Mea saxa,** 'the rocky cave which formed my abode.'

75. **Desertaque conjuge,** sc. *a* conjuge. The preposition is omitted in like manner in Her. 12. 161 :

> *Deseror (amissis regno, patriaque domoque)*
> *Conjuge : qui nobis omnia solus erat.*

76. **Quæque...ferat.** 'And may she herself endure that which she was the first to inflict upon me.'

77-78. If we read 'sequuntur' and 'destituunt,' it will make 'quae' refer to Helen alone, while the subjunctive renders the proposition general, 'such as are ready to follow,' and this seems more appropriate.

Tibi conveniunt. 'Please thee.'

78. **Legitimos toros,** i.e. legitimos viros.

81. **Opes.** 'Wealth.'

85. **Tot.** fifty. Priam when speaking of his sons in his most touching address to Achilles, says—

πεντήκοντά μοι ἦσαν ὅτ' ἤλυθον υἷες Ἀχαιῶν.
'Fifty were mine when came Achaia's sons.'

83. **Non tamen.** 'It must not be supposed, however.' 'Tamen' is used to qualify an expression, to prevent it from being misunderstood, or taken up too strongly. The

pride of Oenone here takes alarm lest her language should be supposed to imply a feeling of unworthiness or unfitness for so high a station.

84. **Dissimulanda,** ' disowned.'

Hecuba. Or Hecûbe, daughter of Dymas or of Cisseus, King of Thrace, wife of Priam. After the fall of Troy she became the slave of Penelope.

85. **Matrona** is always a title of respect—' the wedded wife'—the mother of the family—the mistress of the house.

86. **Quas possint.** ' Quae possint ' is also a legitimate construction.

capit ille coronam
Quae possit crines, Phoebe, decere tuos. Ov. Fast. 2. 106.

' Quas possint decere' is much the same as ' quas deceant,' and this not being understood, gave rise to conjectural emendations on the part of the transcribers, and hence the variations in the text.

91. **Tyndaris.** Gen. Tyndaridis 'daughter of Tyndarus, or Tyndareus' husband of Leda, the mother of Helen.' See Smith's Classical Dictionary.

Fugitivus is the technical term for a runaway slave.

93. **Danais.** ' To the Greeks.' Danus was son of Belus, and founder of Argos. The Greeks engaged in the siege of Troy are often called Danai.

93. **Si.** ' Si' is used for ' num,' a usage sanctioned even by prose writers. Thus Caes. B. G. 1, 8. Saepius noctu, si perrumpere possent, conati.

We have the same idiom in English.

94. Deiphobo. Deiphobus, after Hector, was the best and bravest of all the sons of Priam and Hecuba. We are told in the Odyssey, 8. 517, that his house was stormed at the capture of Troy by Ulysses and Menelaus, and later writers represented him as having wedded Helen after the death of Paris. This account was followed by Virgil, and the student will do well to read the description of the interview between Aeneas and the shade of Deiphobus, in the realms below, Ae. 6. 494.

Polydamanta. Polydămas, son of Panthŏos a Delphian, who had settled at Troy and wedded the niece of Priam, is repeatedly introduced in the Iliad, and represented as one of the wisest, as well as the most valiant, in the Trojan host. With regard to the orthography 'Graece dicitur Πουλύδαμας sed Latinum *Polydamas* priori syllaba longa; formatum est ex Aeolico Πωλύδαμας' R. Hence it is quite unnecessary to write the name 'Pulydamas,' as some desire.

95. Antenor. Antenor, husband of Theano, the sister of Hecuba, is characterized by Homer as an aged, wise, and eloquent counsellor, holding the same position among the Trojans which Nestor occupied among the Greeks. Tradition told, that having escaped from the sack of his native city, he led a band of exiles, who wandered to the head of the Adriatic and founded the city of Patavium. So Virgil, Ae. I. 242.

96. Quis...fuit. 'To whom their long life has been a teacher.'

97. Turpe...raptam. 'It is a base beginning to prefer a woman carried off, to thy country.'

99. **Si sapias.** ' If thou art wise.'

Lacænam. 'The Laconian woman.'

101. **Minor Atrides.** Menelaus, the younger brother of Agamemnon.

104. **Semel,** ' once, and once for all.'

105. **Menelaon.** Greek form of the Acc.

107. **Andromache.** Daughter of Eëtion, and wife of Hector.

Certus maritus is a true and faithful husband opposed to 'incertae nuptiae,' which we find in Ter. And. 5. 1, 11 in the sense of unstable.

109. **Tum cum sine pondere suci.** 'When without the weight of moisture.'

112. **Quae...riget.** 'Which, parched by the constant sunshine, stand stiff in their lightness.'

113. **Recolo,** i.e. in memoriam revoco, animo repeto. The word being somewhat uncommon, gave rise to a multitude of glosses which have crept into the text of different MSS. See various readings.

Germana. i.e. Cassandra, the daughter of Priam and Hecuba, who received from Apollo the gift of prophecy, to which was added the curse that her predictions should never be believed. On the partition of the spoil of Troy, she fell to the lot of Agamemnon, and, on his return home, shared his fate, being murdered by Clytemnestra and her paramour Aegisthus. She plays a prominent part in the noblest production of the Grecian drama, the Agamemnon of Aeschylus. The story of her prophetic powers is unnoticed by Homer.

114. **Diffusis...comis.** 'With dishevelled locks.'

115. **Quid...mandas.** 'Why dost thou commit the seed to the sand ?'

116. **Litora...aras.** A proverbial expression applied to those who waste their toil in endeavouring to effect what can never be accomplished. So Ov. Tr. 5. 4, 47:

> *Plena tot ac tantis referetur gratia factis ;*
> *Nec sinet ille tuos litus arare boves,*

and Juvenal, speaking of the perseverance of unrewarded men of letters,

> *Nos tamen hoc agimus, tenuique in pulvere sulcos*
> *Dueimus, et litus sterili versamus aratro. S. 7. 48.*

117. **Venit,** i.e. **veniet.** This is peculiarly the style of prophets who behold, as it were, the events they describe actually passing before their eyes, as they pour forth the prediction.

'Graia juvenca' is the type under which Cassandra shadows forth Helen in the dark language of prophecy.

119. **Dum licet.** 'While it may be done.'

120. **Obscænam puppim.** The true meaning of 'obscaenus' is 'ill-omened,' and it seems certain that it is connected with 'scaevus,' i.e. 'sinister,' ὁκαιὸς ; thus Virg. G. 1. 470, describing the prodigies which preceded and followed the death of Cæsar,

> *Tempore quamquam illo tellus quoque et aequora ponti,*
> *Obscaenique canes, importunaeque volucres*
> *Signa dabant,*

and in Ae. 12. 876, Juturna exclaims, on seeing the Dira in the shape of a bird, which Jupiter had sent *inque omen Juturnae occurrere jussit,*

> *Jam, jam linquo, acies, ne me terrete timentem,*
> *Obscaenae volucres—* '

hence, it sometimes means simply 'loathsome,' and in that sense is appropriated twice in Ae. 3. 241, and 262 to the Harpies.

121. **In cursu**, i.e. in medio cursu, in ipso furoris impetu, ' while her frenzy was in mid career.'

'Imperaverat Priamus, ut quoties Cassandra solveret os in oracula, toties eam famulae coercerent ut insanam. Meminit Lycophron et ejus interpres' Parrhasius. If we read 'incursu,' it will mean ' the attendants rushing in,' or ' rushing upon her.'

122. **Deriguere**. 'Stood on end.'

126. **Socios...deos**. ' Deos conjugales intelligit' Heins.

128. **Nescio quis Theseus.** ' Oenone, ut mulier pere-grina, fingit se non satis nosse Theseum' R. The story, as narrated by Apollodorus, is simply this. The fame of Helen's beauty being bruited abroad over Greece, Theseus, assisted by Pirithous, bore her away by force and transported her to Athens. He then descended to the infernal regions for the purpose of aiding his friend to carry off Proserpine. Meanwhile Castor and Pollux made war against Athens, captured the city, recovered their sister, and, in retaliation, led prisoner to Sparta, Aethra, the mother of Theseus. The details are given at length in Diodorus and Plutarch. Herodotus also refers to the invasion of Attica by the Tyn-

darids on account of Helen.   Some critics cavil at the
epithet 'juvene,' in v. 129, since they ingeniously calculate
that Theseus, at the period in question, must have been at
least fifty years old.   Were this a grave history we might
entertain the objection ; but when urged against a poet
who is celebrating a mythical hero and a legendary tale, it
is sheer nonsense.

131. **Licet.** 'Though.'

134. **Et poteras...tuis.** 'And thou thyself mightest
be deceived, after thine own example.'

135, 138. **Satyri...Faunus.** The Satyrs, who are con-
stantly represented as the attendants of Bacchus, occupied
the same place in Grecian as the Fauns did in the Italian
mythology.   They were rural deities who roamed through
the woods and wilds, dwelling in caves, and endeavouring to
gain the love of the Nymphs.   They were usually represented with horns and the feet of goats, and covered with
long shaggy hair.   The derivation of the word is uncertain ;
but in all probability the Doric $Tίτυρος$, which signifies
a 'he-goat,' is only a dialetic form of $Σάτυρος$.

136. **Quaesierunt.** Note the short penult.

149. **Non est medicabilis.** 'Not to be cured.'

151. **Ipse repertor.** The train of thought is this: ' I[t]
is little wonderful that I, though skilled in the healing art,
should be unable to minister to my own diseased heart,
since even the god of medicine, Apollo himself, became a
shepherd and fed the herds of Admetus, when wounded by
the shafts of Love.'

Ovid here follows Callimachus and Rhianus the Thracian, in assigning love as the cause of the sojourn of Apollo upon earth in the guise of a herdsman.

The more common legend, as given by Euripides and Apollodorus, told that Zeus having destroyed Aesculapius, Apollo, in vengeance, slew the Cyclopes, or their sons, who had forged the thunderbolts, and was sentenced by the king of heaven to serve as bondsman to a mortal for the space of a year. He accordingly entered the service of Admetus, son of Pheres, the king of Pherae in Thessaly, and tended his cattle on the banks of the river Amphrysus.

A third account, that of Alexandrides the Delphian, assigned the slaughter of the Python as the cause of the punishment of Apollo. The whole of these tales, and the authorities for them, will be found enumerated in the Scholium on the first line of that most touching of dramas, the Alcestis of Euripides.

152. **Et e nostro...fuit.** 'And was smitten by the same passion which now consumes me.'

153. **Quod nec...potes.** 'Thou art able to give me an aid, which neither the earth, so fruitful in producing plants, can give, nor yet the Divinity.'

VARIOUS READINGS.

2. 'litera scripta.' S. 'indignæ' B, 'indigno,' 'indigna.' 11. The best MSS. 'adsit,' some 'absit,' and so L. 16. The best MSS. have either 'Depressa' or 'Deprensa;' 'Defensa' is a conj. of Parrhasius, adopted by B. 20. The best MSS. 'summa;' many have 'longa,' and so B. 24.

' recta meos' in many MSS., and so B.   25.   Twenty-three MSS. have 'consita rivo ;' others 'conscia rivo.'   28. Several MSS. ' numen habes.'   31. Eight MSS. ' recurrite Nymphae.'   33. Many MSS. 'mihi duxit.'   40. 'Grand-aevos.'   41. Four MSS. ' classe peracta,' and so B.   45. ' et madidos vidisti.'   Ib. flentes ocellos.'   48. One good MS. 'vincta,' which is probably a gloss.   49. ' cum te vento' B.   53. ' Phrygio pendentia.'   59. Santenius conj. ' Votis ecce meis.'   69. One MS. 'morabor.'   71. Two MSS. ' Tunc flevi.'   72. Two MSS. ' comas.'   73. 'Idam.'   74. ' Illic,' 'Illinc' B.   77. Many MSS. 'Nunc tecum veniunt.' 77, 88. ' sequuntur,' ' destituunt.'   78. Many MSS. ' viros,' instead of ' toros.'   85. Many MSS. omit ' et,' one has ' potenti.' 86. ' quae possint,' ' quas possunt,' ' quae possent sceptra tenere,' ' quas deceat sceptra tenere.'   94. Some edd. ' Pulydamanta.'   95. Most MSS. ' suadeat,' and so L. 99. ' si cupias.'   111. One MSS. ' levius est in te.' (!)   113. ' nam refero,' ' memoro,' ' memini,' ' repeto.' 116. 'bubus.' 118. ' Perdet.'   119. · Dimergite,' ' demergite.'   121. ' in-cursu.'   125. One MS. 'praesignis,' which is preferred by H. 126. B. has 'patrios—deos' against all the MSS.   128. ' arte.' 131. Many MSS. ' celes.'   136. Most MSS. ' Quae-sierant.'   138. ' et immensis.'   141. B. reads ' medenti,' the conj. of H.   143. Many MSS. ' sanabilis herbis.'   150 ' Destituor.'   152. ' e nostro,' ' Dicitur et nostro.'

ABBREVIATIONS.

B.....................Burmann.
L......................Loers.
K.....................Krebs.
H.................. ....Heinsius.

This epistle is supposed to be addressed by Laodamia, daughter of Acastus, to her husband Protesilaus, who, having determined to take part in the expedition against Troy, had repaired to Aulis in Bœotia, which is named by Homer as having been the gathering-place of the Grecian fleet. Later poets told that the ships were long detained in that harbour by an adverse wind, raised by Artemis in vengeance for the death of a consecrated stag slain by Aga. memnon, and that they were unable to set forth till the wrath of the goddess was at length appeased by the sacrifice of Iphigenia, daughter of the guilty chief.

Laodamia (*Λαοδάμεια*).—Daughter of Acastus, and wife of Protesilaus. When her husband was slain before Troy, she begged the gods to be allowed to converse with him for only three hours. The request was granted. Hermes led Protesilaus back to the upper world, and when Protesilaus died a second time, Laodamia died with him. A later tradition states that Laodamia made an image of her husband, to which she paid divine honours ; but as her father Acastus interfered, and commanded her to burn the image, she herself leaped into the fire and expired.

Protesilao (*Πρωτεσιλάω*).—Protesilaus was the son of Iphiclus and Astyoche. His native place was Phylăce, in Thessaly ; hence he is called Phylacīdes. He sailed for Troy with forty ships, according to Homer, and brought with him many Thessalian warriors. He was the first of all the Greeks who was killed by the Trojans, being the

first who landed on the Trojan shore. According to the
common tradition, he was slain by Hector. Protesilaus is
most celebrated in ancient story for the strong affection
existing between him and his wife Laodamia. His tomb
was shewn near Eleus, in the Thracian Chersonese, where
a magnificent temple was erected to him.

1. **Mittit**, fr. *mitto*, 'I make to go,' 'I send,' causa-
tive form of *meo*, I go. The order of these first two involved
lines is : *Laodamia, amans Haemonis, mittit salutem viro
Haemonio et optat ire, quo mittitur [salus]*. Another interpretation makes *ire = pervenire*, and understands *salutem*
before it ; i.e., *wishes the letter (salutem) to arrive* at the
place *whither it is sent*. Not so good.

Optat [Gr. ὄπτω] governs *ire*.

Salutem [fr. *salvus*]—*Salus*, a wish for one's welfare, ex-
pressed vivâ voce or in writing ; here, in writing, and hence
salutem (pars pro toto) here = *epistolam*.

2. **Haemonis-idis**, adj. fem. = *Thessalis*. Thessaly was
called Haemonia, from Haemonia, one of the daughters of
Deucalion, who gave her name to that district.

3. **Aulide.**—*At* a place of the third declension is put in
the ablative. Aulis, a sea-port town of Bœotia, where the
Greeks were detained by stress of weather, through the
anger of Diana on account of a stag slain by the uncon-
scious Agamemnon, who had to immolate his daughter
Iphigenia to appease the offended deity.

Est fama [fr. *fari*, as φάμα fr. φημί] 'There is a rumor.'

4. **Hic...ventus**, 'Where was this wind ?' *i e.* which
would have detained you at home with me. *Fugeres*, said
reproachfully.

5. 'Then ought the seas to have opposed thy oars.'

Freta.—*Frētum* originally meant a *sound* or *channel*; afterwards used for *the sea.*

Distinguish *frĕta* and *frēta.*

Vestris remis, 'the oars of your crew.' *Remis*, dative after *obsistere.*

6. **Illud...aquis.** 'That was the proper season for the waves to be boisterous.'

Sævus means 'roused to fierceness;' *ferus*, 'naturally fierce.'

7. **Dedissem.** 'I would have given;' plura, 'many a' or 'many.'

Mandata, [*in manus-do*, I give in charge] 'injunctions,' *i.e.*, to take care of yourself, &c.

8. **Plura.** 'Many things.'

9. **Raptus** [Gr. ἁρπαζω.] *Hinc*, i.e., from Phylāce, in Thessaly.

Præceps [*præ-caput, head foremost*] 'in precipitate haste.' *Tua vela vocaret*, 'invited your sails,' *i.e.*, persuaded you to set off.

9. **Et qui...ventus erat.** 'And the breeze which invited thy sails, was such as the mariners desired, not I.'

10. **Nautæ,** contracted form of *navitæ*, [navis, ναῦς] dat. com.

11. **Aptus,** from an obsolete verb, *apo*, [Gr. ἅπτω, to fit] 'suited to,' 'favorable for.'

12. **Amplexus**, 'embrace,' fr. *amplector*, am = ἀμφι (cìr-cum) plecti = πλέκεσθαι, *to twine round* a person.

Solvor. 'I was torn.'

14. **Vale** is a noun here.

15. **Incubuit** ' pressed upon,' *i.e.*, blew violently. *Boreas* [Βορέας] would be the favorable wind to convey him from Thessaly to Aulis. *Abrepta [ab rapio.]*

16. **Jam,** ' Already ' denotes the swiftness of the action.

17. **Juvabat**, gov. *me* understood.

19. **Ut...non poteram.** *Ut* has force of *quum*. 'When I was no longer able.'

20. **Vultus meos,** 'my longing gaze.' *Vultus*, the counte-nance as to *features* and *expression*, frequently meaning ' angry looks ;' *facies*, the *face*.

22. **Et quod....erat.** ' And there was nothing but sea for me to behold.'

Pontus, [Gr. πόντος] 'the open sea.'

23. **Tenebris obortis,** abl. abs. *Tenebræ*, ' the darkness or dimness of a swoon.' *Obortis*, fr. *oborior* [Gr. ὄρνυμι, ὄρω, Eng. *arise*].

24. **Succiduo genu.** ' With tottering knees.'

Succiduo [*sub*, from under, *cado.*] *Dicor*, because in swooning her senses left her ; she can therefore only speak from what her friends told her. *Genu,* Gr. γόνυ, Eng. *knee.*

25. **Iphiclus,** son of Phylacus, and father of Protesilaus. *Grandævus [grande-ævum].*

Acastus. Acastus, father of Laodamia, is usually identified with Acastus, son of Pelias, king of Thessaly. He was one of the Argonauts, and subsequently drove Jason and Medea from Iolcos, after they had compassed the death of his sire. Various other exploits of this hero are enumerated by Apollodorus and others, but they possess no particular interest.

26. **Refecit,** ' restored me.'

27. **Pium,** not *pious,* but *affectionate.*

28. **Miseræ,** dat. after *licuisse.*

29. **Pariter,** ' as well.'

31. **Pectendos,** ' to be arranged,' by my tire-woman.

32. **Capillos,** [*caput*] ' tresses.'

32. **Aurata,** [*aurum*] ' inwoven with gold.'

33. **Ut quas,** ' *Like* [the Bacchantes] *whom.*'

Pampinea...hasta, ' the thyrsus, or magic wand of Bacchus, generally a spear-staff, round which vine-leaves were entwined. *Bicorniger* [bis, cornua, gero], ' the two-horned god.' Bacchus was frequently represented with horns.

34. **Huc illuc...eo.** '*So* do I go to and fro, whither madness impels me."

35. **Matres Phylaceides.** ' Phylaceis ' is a feminine adjective formed from ' Phylace.' Four towns bore this name, one in Thessaly, a second in Macedonia, a third in Epirus, and a fourth in Arcadia ; of these, the first was the abode of Protesilaus and Laodamia. Hence the shade of Protesilaus is called by Statius *Phylaccis umbra.*

36. Indue...sinus. 'Put on, Laodamia, thy royal attire.'

Laodamia, from λάος, δαμάω, like Protesilaus, from πρῶτος, λάος, both indicate an aristocratic or regnant class. Hyginus says Protesilaus was so called because he was the first of all the people to land.

37. Scilicet, 'I suppose, forsooth!' *Murice,* 'purple;' properly, a shell-fish, murex, from which a purple dye was extracted. *Gerere vestes,* 'to wear clothes.' *Gerere bella,* 'to wage war.'

37. Saturatas. '*Lana* saepe dicitur *colorem bibere* vel *sorbere,* quae vero plene et penitus tincta est, proprio verbo dicitur *saturari*' R.

'Murex,' 'Ostrum,' 'Buccina,' 'Conchylium,' 'Purpura,' are the names of shell-fish from which the red liquor, which formed the principal ingredient of the purple dye, was obtained, and hence, each of these words, and the adjectives formed from them, are used for the dye itself.

38. Bella geret, antithetical to *geram vestes.*

Iliacis, 'Trojan.' Distinguish *moenia* and *murus.*

39. Comas pectar. 'Shall I myself have my hair arranged;' *lit.* 'be combed (as to) my hair.' An elegant Græcism. Some, however, read *pectam. Galea,* 'helmet,' usually of leather, whereas the *cassis* is of metal-plate; neither of them a very comfortable head-piece.

40. Novas vestes, opposed to *dura arma,* and governed by *ferat.* The balance of antitheses in this and the preceding lines is very fine.

41. Qua possum, 'as far as I can.' *Qua*, sc. *via*. Others have *quo*, sc. *squalore*. *Squalor*, 'neglect of personal appearance.'

42. Tristis agam, 'I will pass in mourning.'

43. Dyspari, if not the true reading, deserves to be so, being infinitely superior to ' Dux Pari.' It is the Homeric *Δύσπαρι*, i.e., O male et infelix Pari, which occurs Il. 3· 39 ; 13, 769,

Δύσπαρι, εἶδος ἄριστε γυναιμανές ἠπεροπευτά,

Dyspari Priamide, 'Ill-fated Paris, Priam's son !' Both Greek vocatives fr. *Dysparis, idos,* and *Priamides, æ*, Gr. patronymic, from *Πριαμίδης-ου*. The Greek *Δύς* in composition has the force of *malum* as well as *infelix*.

Damno, dat. *incommodi*. *Formosæ* = εἶδος αριστε, Hom.

44 Sis, with optative force, 'mayest thou.'

Hos-tis, hos-pes.—*Hospes* is akin to *hostis*, primarily a stranger, = a stranger who is treated as a guest.

Iners, 'cowardly.'—*Malus* means ' cowardly ' as well as 'evil.' Paris was the guest of Menelaus just before he eloped with Helen.

45. Aut te...tuam. ' Either I could have wished that thou hadst disliked the form of the Taenarian wife, or that thy own had been displeasing to her.'

Tænarum (now *Cape Matapan*), a promontory of Laconia, and the southernmost point of Peloponessus. *Tænaria*, adj. poet. for *Græca*.

4

Culpasse, contr. for *culpavisse,* 'had found fault with.' Laodamia thus reasons : If Paris had not admired Helen, he would not have loved her, would not have carried her off; if she had not been captivated by his personal attractions (*formosus,* v. 43), she would not have eloped with him; there would have been no war, and my husband would have been at home with me.

47. **Pro rapta.** 'To recover your runaway wife.'

Nimium, 'excessively—much more than she is worth.'

48. **Flebilis,** i.e. lacrimarum causa. So Amor. 2. 1, 32, *Raptus et Hæmoniis flebilis Hector equis.*

49. **Sinistrum,** 'inauspicious.' Laodamia deprecates the wrath of the gods for having said *multis flebilis,* and hopes her fears may prove unfounded. The use of ' omen *sinistrum*' here is very appropriate, coming from a Greek; for, in auspices and divinations, the Romans turned the face towards the south, and so had the eastern, or fortunate, side on their left ; while the Greeks, turning to the north, had it on their right.

50. **Det,** 'offer up.' **Reduci...Jovi,** ' To Jupiter who restored him in safety.' It was customary for returning warriors to hang up their armour in the temples, and offer sacrifices for their safe return. Distinguish *redŭci* [redux] and *redūci.*

52. **More...eunt.** 'My tears flow just like the snow when heated by the sun.'

More, abl. of *manner.*

53. **Ilion...Simoisque.** Ilion or Troy received many names from its different kings. It was called *Troja* from Tros, son of Ericthonius, and grandson of Dardanus : *Teucria* from Teucer ; *Dardania* from Dardanus ; *Ilium* or *Ilion* from Ilus. Troy comprised all that district to the north-west of Mysia, in Asia Minor, bounded on the west by the Ægean Sea, on the north by the Hellespont, on the east by the mountains which border on the valley of the Rhodius, and on the south by the Gulf of Adramyttium. The territory of Troy, properly called the Troad, is for the most part mountainous, being intersected by Mount Ida and its branches ; the largest plain is that in which the city of Troy stood. The chief rivers were the Satnioeis on the south, the Rhodius on the north, and the Simois and Scamander in the centre. These two rivers, so renowned in the legends of the Trojan war, flow from two different points in the chain of Mount Ida, and unite in the plain of Troy, through which the united stream flows north-west, and falls into the Hellespont east of the promontory of Sigeum.

Tenedos, an island off the coast of Troy. *Xanthus,* a river, and *Ide,* a mountain of Troy.

55. **Nec rapere ausurus...hospes erat,** ' nor was the stranger (Paris) likely to dare to run off,' with Helen.

56. **Noverat,** fr. nosco ; old form, *gnosco,* Eng. *know.*

57. **Spectabilis,** ' an object of wonderment' to the frugal Spartan people. *Auro,* abl. of *cause.*

58. ' A prince who carried about on his person the wealth of Phrygia.'

59. Classe virisque, 'army and navy.' *Potens*, supply *venerat.* Per *quæ*, some read *per quos*, referring to viris.

60. Quota pars. 'How small a part.'

61. His, i.e., by Paris's brilliant display and well-appointed retinue. *Victam* (*esse*).

Consors Ledæa gemellis. The 'gemelli' are Castor and Pollux, twin sons of Leda, and brothers of Helena and Clytemnestra. 'Consors' is frequently applied by Ovid in an extended signification to brothers and sisters.

Ledæa, 'daughter of Leda.'

62. Danais, dat. *incom.*—The Greeks were called Danai, from Danaus, son of Belus, and brother of Aegyptus, who wandered out of Egypt into Greece, and there founded Argos.

Danais nocere, 'to work the Greeks woe.'

63. Hectora... nescio quem, 'one Hector;' lit. 'Hector. I know not who he may be." Paris had been boasting in Greece of Hector's martial prowess. This was all Laodamia knew about him, but she had fearful misgivings of some mishap befalling her husband by Hector's hands. Her worst fears were realized, for, as we have seen above, Protesilaus fell by the bloody hand (*sanguinea manu*) of Hector.

64. Ferrea, 'cruel.'

65. Quisquis is est, si sum. Note the sigmatismus. Euripides is charged with being fond of recurrences of the letter *s* (sigma).

The sibilation in this line would seem to indicate that the Roman ear was not very delicate in these matters.

66. **Signatum...habe.** 'Have his name imprinted on thy mindful breast.'

67. **Vitaris,** contr. for *vitaveris.*

68. **Hectoras,** h. e. multos viros fortes qualis Hector R. So Sueton. Caes. I. *Caesari multos Marios inesse.* It is a very common English idiom.

69. **Facito ut dicas,** i.e., 'Fail not to repeat.'

70. **Parcere sibi.** Laodamia intimates that if her husband perishes she will also die.

71. **Si...fas est.** 'If it be the will of heaven.' 'Fas' properly denotes divine law, while human institutions are called 'jura.'

74. **Ut rapiat...et armis.** 'That he may take from Paris what Paris before took from him. Let him rush on : and him, whom he conquers in the justice of his cause may he conquer, too, in arms !'

74, 75. The genuineness of these two lines has been called in question, in consequence of their being omitted in several MSS. Moreover, 'sibi' is startling, where we should have expected 'illi,' but this difficulty may be explained, by supposing that the speaker puts himself, in fancy, in the place of Menelaus.

77. **Dispar,** 'unlike' that of Menelaus.

77. **Vivere pugna.** 'Pugnare' frequently signifies 'to struggle,' 'to make an effort to attain some object,' and in this sense it is construed with the infinitive by the poets, as in the passage before us.

79. Parcite...uni. 'Spare, O descendants of Dardanus, this one, I beseech you, out of foes so many.'

79. Dardanidæ. By a felicitous turn of the diction, Laodamia apostrophizes the Trojans as if present.

80. Meus...sanguis, 'my life-blood;' because she was so wrapt up in him, that the continuation of her own life depended on his.

81. Non est...viros. 'He is not one whom it becomes to engage with the naked sword, and to present an undaunted breast to the opposing side.'

85, 86. Fateor [cf. Gr. φάω, φημί], 'now I confess, what before I dared not say for fear of using ill-omened speech.

Volui, [akin to βούλομαι] 'I wished to call you back, and my mind was leading me' to recall you. Distinguish *animus, anima,* and *mens.*

86. Substitit, 'stood still.' *Auspicii,* derived from *avis-spicere,* here simply means 'omen;' lit., *augury from birds.*

87. Foribus, fr. foris, Gr. θύρα, Eng. *door.*

88. Pes, pedis, Ger. πούς, ποδός, 'Your foot gave an ill-omen by stumbling on the threshold,' which among the ancients was considered unlucky. *Offenso limine,* abl. abs.; iit., 'the threshold having been struck by it.' No omen was considered more fatal than to stumble over the threshold when setting forth upon a journey, or going in and out upon serious business. For this reason a bride was always carried over the threshold, both when she left the house of her parents and when she entered that of her husband.

91. **Ne sis animosus.** 'Be not too forward,' 'too rash.' 'Animosus' signifies, properly, 'full of spirit,' and therefore, 'brave,' 'intrepid ;' so Ov. T. 4. 6, 3.

92. **Fac...eat.** 'Cause all these apprehensions of mine to vanish in the winds.'

94. **Danaum,** Gen. plur.

Troada. 'Troas,' adj. gen. Troädis, 'Trojan.'

96. **Di faciant.. velis !** 'May the gods grant that thou mayest not desire to be *thus* courageous !'

97. **Mille,** used indefinitely. The exact number given by Homer is 1186.

98. **Fatigatas,** i.e., remis aliorum.

100. If we read 'properas,' the meaning will be, 'the land to which you are hastening is not your native land.' If 'properes,' 'you have no native land to which you can hasten.' The latter sense is manifestly quite inapplicable here.

101. **Cum venies.** 'When thou art returning;' *lit.* 'when thou shalt be returning.'

102. **Siste.** 'Set,' thy foot.

103. **Phœbus.** The *Bright* or *Pure*, an epithet of Apollo. Greek Φοῖβος.

Seu extat. 'Whether he is visible.'

104. **Dolor.** 'An object of care.'

105. **Quarum...habet.** 'Whose neck the arm placed beneath supports.'

107. Aucupor...somnos. 'Aucupor,' properly, 'to watch eagerly,' as a bird-catcher for his prey—and hence, 'to seize eagerly.'

Somnos. 'Dreams.'

108. Veris. 'Real ones.'

111. Simulacra. 'I pay homage to the visions of the night,' i.e., I offer sacrifices in order to propitiate the nocturnal deities by whom these ill-omened dreams (described in the preceding couplet) were sent, and so to avert the evil they threaten.

112. Thessalis. Gen. Thessalĭdis ; adj. fem. 'Thessalian.'

Fumo meo. 'Smoke of my incense.'

113. Qua sparsa...mero. 'Sprinkled with which, the flame burns bright, as it is wont to blaze up, when wine is poured upon it.'

126. Distinguish *paratis* and *parilis*.

126—128. Three ablatives absolute occur in these lines.

Pelago. Gr. πέλαγος. This same sea now bears the name of 'The Archipelago.'

129. Suam. Referring to the legend that the walls of Troy were the work of Neptune and Apollo.

Suam, because Neptune built Troy's walls.

130. Ruitis, *ruo,* Eng. *rush* **Redite,** *redeo ;* fr. *re* and *eo,* with an epenthetic *d.*

131. Vetantes.—An elegant reading is *tonantes.*

132. **Subiti casus,** gen. sing., not nom. pl. Translate :
' This remarkable (*ista*) delay (of your sailing) is not (the
result) of unforeseen chance (but the work) of the deity,' *i.e.*,
of Neptune.

133. **Adultera.**—Helen.

134. **Inachiae rates.** Inachus, the tutelary god of the
stream which bore the same name, and his son Phoroneus,
were the personages to whom the inhabitants of Argolis considered themselves indebted for a knowledge of the useful
arts and the establishment of social order. Hence Inachius
became equivalent to Argivus and so to Graecus. The patronymic Inachides is applied by Ovid both to Epaphus
whom Io daughter of Inachus bore to Jupiter, and also to a
more remote descendant, the hero Perseus, son of Jupiter
and Danaë.

135. The common reading is ' sed qui egō revoco', which
seems corrupt, since ' the poets of the golden age shorten or
elide the final *o* of ego, never make it long.'

137. **Troasin.** ' The Trojan ladies.' Heinsius, offended
by what appeared to him a solecism, conjectures ' Troasin'
the Greek dative plural. Such forms were undoubtedly
used by the Latin poets, for we find ' Dryasin ' and ' Hama-
dryasin ' in Propertius, and ' Arcasin ' is recognised by
Martianus Capella. See ' Various Readings.'

143. **Producet.** ' She will detain.'

Reverti. ' To return.'

144. **Referas...Jovi.** ' Take care and bring back these
arms for Jupiter.'

149. **Nos**, i.e., 'We, Grecian wives, who are so far from our husbands.'

149. **Nos anxius...timor**. 'Anxious apprehensions compel us to fancy everything to be done that can happen.'

151. **Diverso in orbe**. 'In a distant region.'

152. **Quae...tuos**. 'I have a waxen image which recals thy features.'

153. **Illi**. 'To it.'

155. She imagines some mysterious connection or sympathy to exist between Protesilaus and this waxen image.

157. **Hanc specto**. 'At this do I look.'

158. **Et...queror**. 'And, as if it could utter words in answer, do I complain.'

160. **Animi**. 'Of affection.'

161. **Perque....cuput**. 'And by that hand, which mayest thou with thyself restore to me, that I may behold it white, with its hoary locks '

164. **Sive...quod heu timeo...eris**. 'Whether —— which alas I dread, or whether thou shalt be surviving.' A beautiful example of *aposiopesis*, after the first *sive*.

VARIOUS READINGS.

'Aemonis Aemonio' L. 4. Nine MSS. 'A me.' 7. One MS. 'plura meo.' 8. Many MSS. 'multa tibi,' and so L. 13. 'mandatis.' Ib. 'relinquit' B. 14. 'potui' L; others 'volui.' 15. 'abrepta;' 'erepta;' 'afflata.' 23.

'tenebrisque' L. 26. 'membra refecit.' 29. 'Utque
animus rediit.' 35. 'Phylleides' B, the conj. of H;
'Phylaides.' 39. 'pectam.' 38, 39, 40. 'gerat,' 'pre-
matur,' 'ferat,' and so B. 41. 'Quo possum' L. 43.
'Dyspari,' 'Dispari ;' all the rest have 'Dux Pari,' and so
B and L. 49. 'omen revocate.' 51. 'quoties subiit.' 53.
'Ida.' 59. H. conj. 'per quos.' 60. 'quotacunque,'
'quotaquaeque,' and so B, 'quotaquamque.' 65. 'si
quis is est.' Ib. 'tibi cura.' 69. One MS. 'facito dicas,'
and so B. 74, 75. These two lines are wanting in some
MSS. 83 'Fortis ille potest multo qui pugnat amore,'
'cui pugnat ;' H. conj. 'quum pugnat amore,' and so B.
86. 'Sed stetit,' or 'Sed stetit auspiciis lingua retenta
malis.' 89. 'Ut vidi, gemui ;' 'Et vidi et gemui;' H conj.
'Ut vidi, ut gemui,' and so B. 90. 'recursuri.' 94.
'tanget,' 'tangit.' 100. 'properes' B. 111. 'Excitor e
somno.' 113. 'Tura damus lacrimasque super quae sparsa
relucet.' 'Tura damus lacrimamque super qui ora relucet.'
'quaesa relucet' 'quis ara relucet.' 114. 'a fuso ;' others
'effuso.' 116. 'tristitia solvar.' 119. H conj. 'juvant.'
120. 'rapies.' 121. 'narrantis ;' one 'narranti.' 122.
'linguae.' Ib. 'retenta mora' B. 131. 'audite sonantes,'
'tonantes.' 135. 'Sed quid ego revoco haec ? Omen
revocantis abesto,' and so B and L ; or 'Sed quid ego haec
revoco? Omen revocantis abesto.' 137. One MS. has
'Troas ;' all the rest have 'Troadas ;' Salmasius and H
conj. 'Troasin,' and so B. 144. 'face' B. 148. 'pectora'
B. 151. 'geris,' 'geras.' 154. 'illa tuos.' 165. 'claud-
atur.' 166. Almost all MSS. 'Sit—sit,' and so L ; one
has 'Si—si.'

VOCABULARY.

EXPLANATIONS OF ABBREVIATIONS, &c.

cf	compare.	*sing*	singular.
r. a	verb active.	*pl.or plur.*	plural.
v. p	" passive.	*adj*	adjective.
v. n	" neuter.	*comp. adj.*	adjective in the comparative degree.
r. ir	" irregular.		
v. dcp	" deponent.	*subst.*	substantive.
v. imp ...	" impersonal.	*sup. adj.* ..	adjective in the superlative degree.
intens.	intensive.		
s.	substantive.	*num. adj.*	numeral adjective.
ind	indeclinable.	*pro*	pronoun.
m.	masculine.	*part.*	participle.
f.	feminine.	*prep.*	preposition.
fr	from.	*conj*	conjunction.
n.	neuter.	*adv*	adverb.
c.	common.	*etc.*	et cetera.

The figures after the verb show to what conjugation the verb belongs; as 2. *v. a.* VERB ACTIVE of the SECOND conjugation. The *genitives* of *nouns* and the *infinitives* and *perfect tenses* of verbs are given.

N.B. The meanings of the words given are those appropriate to the TEXT, and not always the usual and most general significations.

Ā. See ab.

Ab. (ā), prep. gov. abl.: 1. *From, away from.* — 2. *From, down from.*—3. In time: *After.*—4. *From, on account of, in consequence of.* — 5. To denote the agent: *By, by means of* [akin to Gr. *α'π-ó*].

Ab-ĕo, īvi *or* ĭi, ĭtum, īre, v. n. [ăb, ĕo]. *To go away* or *depart.*

Ab-sum, fŭi, esse, v. n. [ăb. 'away from;' sum, 'to be']. 1. *To be away from* a place *or* person ; *to be absent* or *distant.*—2. *To be wanting, to be free* from.

Abĭes, ĕtis, f. *A pine tree ; a fir.*

Abreptus, a, um, *part. from abripio.*

Abripio, pui, eptum, 3 v. a. [ab, 'from ;' rapio, 'to

snatch']. *To drag away, to hurry away.*

Acastus, i, m. Son of Pelias, King of Thessaly, husband of Astydamia, and father of Laodamia.

Ac-cĭpĭo, cēpi, ceptum, cĭpĕre. 3. v. a. [for ad-căpĭo.] 1. *To take, receive.—2. To perceive, hear, learn.—* Pass.: ac-cĭpĭor, ceptus sum, cĭpi.

Ădōro, āvi, ātum. 1. v. a. *To speak to, entreat, adore.*

Ăcūtus, a, um, adj. [ăcŭo, 'to sharpen']. *Sharp, pointed, clear.*

Ad, prep. gov. acc. *To, towards.*

Addo, dĭdi, dĭtum, ĕre. 3. v. a. *To add.*

Ademptus, a, um, P. perf. pass. of ădĭmo.

Adfundo, fūdi, fūsum. 3. v. a. *To pour to or upon.*

Adfūsus, a, um, *part of adfundo.*

Ad-ĭmo, ēmi, emptum, imĕre, 3. v. a. [for ăd-ĕmo; fr. ăd, 'to;' ĕmo, 'to take']. *To take away from another; to deprive another of.—*Pass.:ăd-ĭmor, emptus, sum, ĭmi.

Admitto, mīsi, missum, 3. v. a. *To admit.*

Ădvĕho, xi, ctum. 3. v. a. *To bring to.*

Adver-sus, sa, sum, adj. [fr. advert-o, 'to turn towards']. *Opposite, adverse.*

Adultĕra, ae, f. *An adulteress.*

Æqu-or, ŏris, n. [æqu-o, 'to make level']. 1. *The smooth surface of the sea.* —2. (Sometimes plur.): *The sea.*

Æquŏrĕus, a, um, adj. *Of the sea* [æquor, 'the sea'].

Æ-tas, tātis. f. [fr. æv-um, 'life, age']. *Time, or season, of life; age.*

Ăgo, ēgi, actum, ăgĕre, 3. v. a. 1. *To drive.—2. To chase, pursue.—3. To effect, do.—4. To plead.— 5. To enjoy.--6. Of thanks: to return.--7. Of feasts: to keep.* Res agendae = *business.*—Pass.; ăgor, actus, sum, ăgi.

Ah, interj. *Ah! Alas!*

Alb-ĕo, no perf. nor sup., ēre, 2. v. n. [alb-us, 'white']. *To be white.*

Al-ĭus, ĭa, ĭud (Gen. ălīus: Dat. ălĭi), adj. *Another, other* [akin to Gr. αλ-λος].

Al-tus, ta, tum, adj. [ăl-o, 'to nourish ']. (a) *High, lofty.* As Subst : altum, i, n. *A lofty place or spot.* —(b) *Aloft, on high.— Deep.* Comp. : alt-ĭor.

Amīca, ae, f. *A female friend, a mistress* [amo, 'to love'].

Am-o, āvi, ātum, āre, 1. v. a. *To love.* Si quis amas = *If you love, or take a pleasure in.*

Ăm-or, ōris, m [am-o, 'to love']. 1. *Love.*—2. *A beloved object, a love.*

Amplexus, ūs, m. [amplector, 'to twine around']. *An encircling, an embrace, caress.*

Au. conj. [prob. a primitive word]. 1. Introducing the second half of a disjunctive sentence : *Or:*—an . . . an, *whether* . . *or.*— 2. *Whether or not.* — 3. With utrum to be supplied in first clause : (*Whether*) *or.*

Andrŏmăchē, ēs, f. *The wife of Hector.*

Anĭmōsus, a, um, adj. [animus, 'courage']. *Courageous, bold, spirited.*

An-ĭmus, ĭmi, m 1. *The rational soul in man; mind.* -2. *Disposition, character.* —3. *Courage, heart, spirit* [akin to Gr. ἄνεμος, 'a stream of air'].

An-nus, ni, m.: *A year* [akin to Gr. εν-νος = εν-ιαυτος, 'a year'].

Ante, adv. and prep.: 1. Adv.: (a) *Before, in front.* —(b) In time: (a) *First.*— (b) *Before, previously.*— 2. Prep. gov. acc. *Before, in front of.* [Gr. ἀντί.]

Antenor, ŏris, m. *A noble Trojan.*

Ănus, ūs, f. *An old woman.*

Anxĭus, a, um, adj. [ango, 'to bind']. *Anxious, solicitous, uneasy.*

Apertus, a, um, adj. [ăpērio, 'to open']. *Open, clear.*

Appello, āvi, ātum, 1 v. n. and a. *To approach, accost, name, call.*

Appōno, pŏsŭi, pŏsĭtum, 3. v. a. *To place near, unite.*

Appŏsĭtus, a, um, part. oj *appono.*

Apte, ad. *Closely, fitly, suitably.*

Ap-tus, ta. tum, adj. [obsol. ăp-ĭo, 'to lay hold of']. With Inf. : *Suited, adapted; ready,* of a sword.

Aqu-a, æ, f. ; 1. *Water.*— 2. *The water, the waters.*

Ar-a (old form ās-a), æ, f. *An altar.*

Arbitrĭum, ii, n [arbĭter, 'a master']. *Will, pleasure.*

Arbos, or, arbor, ŏris, f. *A tree.*

Ardĕo, arsi, arsum, 2.v. n *To burn or be inflamed*

Arēna, æ, f. [ārĕo, 'to be dry']. *Sand.*

Arĭdus, a, um, adj, [ārĕo, 'to be dry']. *Dry.*

Arista, æ. f. *The top, awn, or beard of an ear of grain.*

Ar-ma, mōrum, n. plur. *Arms, weapons* [akin to ἄρ-ω, 'to adapt'].

Armentum-i, n, [ăro, 'to plough']. *Cattle, a drove, a herd.*

Aro, āvi, ātum, 1. v. a. *To plough* (αροω).

Ar-s, tis, f. 1. *Art, skill.* 2. *Science, knowledge.*—3. *Stratagem, device, artifice.* —4. *Business* [akin to ἄρ-ω, 'to join'].

A-spĭcĭo, spexi, spectum, spĭcĕre, 3. v. a. : [fr. ăd, spĕcĭo]. *To look on or upon ; to behold, see.*

Assiduus, a, um, adj. [assideo, 'to be continually somewhere']. *Continual, perpetual.*

At, conj. *But* [akin to Gr. ἀτ-ἀρ, 'but'].

Atrīdes, æ, m   A male descendant of Atreus.

Attonītus, a, um, adj. [attŏno, 'to thunder at']. *Inspired, frantic.*

Attingo, tĭgi, tactum, 3. v. a. [ad.: tango, 'to touch']. *To touch against, attain to, arrive at.*

Aucŭpor, ātus, 1. v. dep. a. [auceps-cŭpis, 'a bird-catcher']. *To go fowling, chase, pursue.*

Audio, īvi, ītum, 4. v. a. *To hear.*

Aufĕro, abstŭli, ablatum, auferre, v. a. [ab. : fero, 'to bear']. *To carry off, or away, to snatch away.*

Aulis, ĭdis or is, f.   A sea-port town in Bœotia, from which the Grecian fleet set sail for Troy.

Aura, æ, f. *The air, a breeze.*

Aurātus, a, um, adj. [aurum, 'gold']. *Gilded, gilt, adorned with gold.*

Auspĭcĭum, ii, n. [auspex]. An *omen* from birds, *auspices.*

Aut, conj. : *Or:*—aut.. aut, *either .. or.*

Auxilium, i, n. [augeo, 'to increase']. *Aid, help.*

Barbărus, a, um, adj. *Foreign, strange, barbarous.*

Bellum, li, n. [old form dū-ellum ; fr. dŭ-o, 'two']. *War, warfare.*

Bĕnĕ, adv. *Well.*

Bĭcornĭger, ĕri [bis, 'twice,' cornu, 'a horn,' gero, 'to bear']. *Two-horned.*

Blandītĭa, æ, f. [blandus, 'flattering']. *A caressing, fondling.*

Blandus, a, um, adj. *Charming, soft.*

Bŏnus, a, um, adj. *Good pious.* Comp. : mĕlĭor.

Bŏrĕas, æ. m.   *The north wind, the north.*

Bos, bŏvis (Plur. bŏves, bŏum), comm. gen. *A cow* or *ox ;*—Plur. : *Cattle* [akin to Greek Βοῦς].

Brāchĭum, ĭi, n. *An arm* [akin to Βραχιων].

Cădo, cĕcĭdi, cāsum, cădĕre, 3. v. n. *To fall.*

Caedo, cĕcīdi, caesum, 3. v. a. *To cut, to slaughter, vanquish, slay.*

Caelebs, ībis. *Unmarried, single.*

Caerŭlus, a, um, adj. [caesius, 'bluish gray']. *Dark blue, azure.*

Cāneo, ui, 2. v. n. *To be gray or hoary.*

Cănis, is, c. *A dog.*

Cāno, cĕcĭni, cantum, cănĕre, 3. v. n. and a. : 1. Neut.: *To sing;* 2. Act.: *To celebrate,* or *praise, in song.*

Cānus, a, um, adj. *Gray, hoary, white.*

Căp-illus, ĭlli, m. *The hair* of the head[akin to cap-ut, Gr. κεφ-αλή].

Căpĭo, cēpi, captum, căpĕre. 3. v. a.: *To take, to capture, to receive, contain.* Pass.: căpĭor, captus sum căpi.

Căput, ĭtis, n. [κεφαλή, cf. Ger. Kopf]. *The head.*

Căr-ĕo, ŭi, ĭtum, ēre, 2. v. n With Abl. 1. *To be without, not to have, to fail of.*—2. *To be deprived of, to want* [akin κείρ-ω, 'to shear '].

Cărīna, æ, f. *The keel of a ship, a ship, vessel.*

Car-men, mĭnis, n. 1. *A poem, poetry.*—2. *A song* or *strain.*

Cā-rus, ra, rum, adj. *Be-* loved, dear. Comp.: cārĭor : Sup.: cār-issĭmus.

Că-sa, sæ, f. *A hut, cottage, cabin,* etc.

Castus, ta, tum, adj. *Chaste, pure* [akin to Gr. καθ-αρός, 'pure '].

Cāsus, us, m. [cădo, 'to fall ']. *A falling, accident, chance.*

Cătŭlus, i, m. *A hound, dog.*

Causa, æ, f. *A cause, a reason, origin.*

Caute, adv. [cautus, 'cautious']. *Cautiously, carefully.*

Cĕlĕber, bris, bre, adj. *Celebrated.*

Celer, ĕris, ĕre, adj. [cello, 'to urge on']. *Swift, rapid, quick.*

Cēra, æ, f. 1. *Wax.*—2. *A waxen image,* of ancestors [akin to κηρ-ός].

Cērātus, a, um, *part. of* cēro.

Cēro, āvi, ātum, 1. v. a. [cēra, 'wax']. *To smear with wax.*

Certe, adv. [cerno, 'to separate']. *Surely, certainly.*

Certus, a, um, adj. [cerno, 'to decide']. *Sure, certain.*

Cĭtus, a, um, adj. *Quick, swift, rapid* [cieo, 'to move '].

Clāmo, āvi, ātum, 1.v.n. *To call, complain* (καλέω).

Classis, is, f. *A fleet.*

Clau-do, si, sum, dĕre, 3. v.
a. *To shut, to shut up,
shut in, enclose.*—Pass. :
clau-dor, sus sum, di [akin
to κλει-ω, 'to shut'].

Clypĕus, i, m. [καλύπτω,
'to cover']. *A shield.*

Cito, adv. (cĭtus). *Quickly,
soon.*

Cĭtus, a, um, adj. [cĭĕo, 'to
put in motion']. *Swift,
rapid, quick.*

[Coepio], coepi, coeptum, 3.
v. a. *To begin.*

Co-gnosco, gnōvi, gnĭtum.
gnoscĕre, 3. v. a. [co (=
cum), gnosco = nosco]. *To
become well acquainted
with :* in Perf. tenses. *to
have knowledge of, to know.*
Pass. : co-gnoscor, gnĭtus
sum, gnosci.

Cōgo, cōēgi, cŏactum, cō-
gĕre, 3. v. a. [contr. fr.
cŏ-ăgo; fr. co (=cum),
'together ;' ăgo, 'to
drive']. *To compel, force,
constrain.*

Collum, i, n. *The neck.*

Cŏma. æ, f. *The hair* (κόμη).

Cŏm-e-s, cŏmitis, comm gen.
[fr. com. (=cum, 'to-
gether ;' ĕo, 'to go'].
1. *A companion.*—2. *An
attendant* on a person.

Compĕrĭo, peri, pertum, 4.
v. a. [pario, 'to bring
forth']. *To find out, to
learn.*

Compōno, pŏsŭi, pŏsĭtum,

3. v. a. *To put together,
compose, quiet.*

Compŏsĭtus, a, um, part.
from compōno.

Concurro, curri, cursum, 3.
v. n. *To run together, to
engage.*

Conjŭgĭum, ii, n. [conjŭgo,
'to join']. *Union, wedlock.*

Conjux, ŭgis, comm. gen.
[for conjug-s]. 1. Of men :
A husband.—2. Of women:
A wife, spouse.— 3. Of
birds : *A mate.*

Consĕro, sēvi, sĭtum, 3. *To
plant.*

Con-sisto, stĭti, stĭtum, sist-
ĕre, 3. v. n. [con (=cum),
insisto]. *To place one's
self, to take up one's abode.*

Consĭtus, a, um, part. of consĕro.

Consors, rtis, adj. [con-sors].
Sharing. As Subst. *part-
ner.*

Con-spĭcĭo, spexi, spectum,
3. v. a. *To see, behold,
observe.*

Conspĭcŭus, a, um, adj. [con-
spicio]. *Conspicuous, distinguished.*

Consto, stĭti, stātum, 1.v.n.
*To stand still, to agree, to
be manifest.*

Consŭlo, ŭi, tum, ĕre, 3. v.
n. and a. *To take counsel
or measures ; to consult.*

Contentus, a, um, adj. [con-
tineo, 'to hold together'].
Content.

Convĕnĭo, vēni, ventum. 4. To come together, to agree with, to please.

Cornĭger, ĕra, ĕrum. adj. [cornu, 'a horn,' gero, 'to carry']. Horned.

Cor, cordis, n. The heart.

Corp-us, ŏris, n. A body.

Cortex-ĭcis, m. and f. The bark of the cork tree, cork.

Crēdo, dĭdi, dĭtum, 3. v. n. and a.: Act. With Objective clause : To believe, or suppose, that; Pass. : crē-dor, dĭtus, sum, di.

Crēdŭlus, a, um, adj. [crēdo, 'to believe']. Believing, confiding, relying on.

Crĕo, āvi, ātum, 1.v. a. To bring forth, produce.

Cresco, crēvi, crētum, ēre, 3. v. n. [creo]. To increase.

Crī-men, mĭnis, n.[probably akin to cerno]. 1. A charge, accusation.—2. A crime, fault, offence,

Crŭentus, a, um, adj. [crŭor, 'blood']. Bloody, cruel.

Culpa, æ, f. [cf. scelus]. A fault.

Culpo, āvi, ātum, 1. v. a. [culpa, 'a fault']. To find fault with, blame.

Cul-tus, tūs, m, [for coltus; fr. cŏl-o, 'to cultivate']. A cultivating ; cultivation, tillage, dress.

Cum, conj.i.q. quum. When.

Cum. prep. gov. abl. With, together with. [Gr. ξυν, σuν].

Cŭpĭdus, a, um, adj. [cupio, 'to desire']. Desirous of, eager for.

Cŭpĭo, ĭvi or ii, ītum, 3. v. a. To desire, long for.

Cur, adv.[contr. fr. qua re, or cui rei]. Why, wherefore.

Curro, cŭcurri, cursum, currēre, 3. v. n. 1. To run. 2. Of streams: To run, flow.

Cursus, us, m. [curro, 'to run']. Running, journey, march, voyage.

Dam-num, ni. n. Hurt, harm, damage, injury, loss [akin Gr. δαμ-άω, 'to tame'],

Dănăi, ōrum, m. plur. The Greeks.

Dardănĭdes, æ, m. Descendant of Dardanus, in the plur. Trojans.

Dē, prep. gov. abl. : 1. From, away from.—2. From, down from.—3. From, or out of : From, by, by means of.

Dēbĕo, ui, ĭtum, 2.v. a. [dehabeo, 'to have']. To have from, to owe.

Dĕcens, ntis, adj. [dĕcet, 'it becomes']. Comely, graceful.

Dĕcet, ŭit, 2. v. n. and a. Is becoming or proper, becomes, suits.

Dēfendo, di, sum, ĕre. 3. v. a. To defend.

Dēfensus, a, um, part. from
dēfendo.

Dēfĭcĭo, fēci, fectum, ēre, 3.
v. n.   To fail.

Dēïphŏbus, i, m.   A son of
Priam.

Dēmergo, mersi, mersum,
3. v. a. [de; mergo, 'to
plunge']. To plunge down
into, overwhelm in.

Dēnĭ-que, adv. [fr. dĕin,
'then ;' quĕ, 'and ']. 1.
At length, at last.—2. In
a word, in short, briefly.

Depereo, ii, 4. v. n.   To
perish, be lost.

Dērĭgesco, gŭi, 3.v. inch. n.
To become wholly stiff, or
rigid.

Dē-sĕro, sĕrŭi, sertum, sĕr-
ēre, 3. v. a. [dē, sēro].   To
forsake, abandon, desert.—
Pass. : dē-sĕror, sertus
sum, sĕri.

Designo, āvi, ātum, 1. v. a.
To mark out.

Despĭcĭo, spexi, spectum, 3.
v. a.   To look down.

Dēstĭtŭo, ŭi, ūtum, 3. v. a.
[statuo, 'to place'].   To
set down, forsake, desert.

Dētĭnĕo, ŭi, entum, 2. v. a.
[de; teneo, 'to hold'].   To
hold back, detain.

Dĕus. i (Nom. plur. dî), m.
A god, deity [akin to Gr.
θεύς].

Dīco, dixi, dictum, dicĕre,
3. v. a.   1. To say.—2

To tell of, declare, men-
tion, etc.—3. To speak,
utter.   Pass. : dicor, dic-
tus sum, dīci [akin to Gr.
δεἱϰ-νυμι].

Dĭes, ēi, m. (in sing. sometimes f.)   A day, time.

Diffūsus, a, um, adj. [diffun-
do, 'to scatter']. Dishe-
velled.

Dig-nus. na, num, adj. With
Abi. : Worthy or deserving
of [akin to dic-o].

Dīmissus, a, um, part. of
dimitto.

Dīmitto, mīsi, missum, 3.
v. a.   To send apart, separate, dismiss.

Dī-rus, ra, rum, adj. Fearful,
terrible, dire, appalling
[prob. akin to δεἱ-δω,
'to fear '].

Dis-cūdo, cessi, cessum, cēd-
ēre, 3. v. n. [dis cēdo].
To go away, depart.

Dispar, ăris, adj.   Unlike,
different.

Displĭceo, ŭi, ĭtum, 2. v. n.
[dis ; placeo, 'to please'].
To displease.

Dissĭmŭlo, āvi, ātum, 1.v.a.
[dissĭmĭlis, 'unlike']. To
dissemble, disguise, keep
secret, disown.

Distinctus, a, um, part. of
distinguo.

Distingŭo, nxi, nctum, 3.v.
a.   To separate, decorate,
adorn.

Dīver-sus, sa, sum, adj. [dī-

vert-o]. 1. *Turned away.*
—2. *Different, diverse.*
Dĭu, adv. [old abl. form of
dies, 'a day']. *For a long
time, long.*
Do, dĕdi, dătum, dăre. 1.
v. a. : 1. *To give* in the
widest acceptation of the
term. —2. *To allot, assign.*
—3. *To supply, furnish.*—
4. Of a sound ; *To give
forth.*—5. Of a favour,
etc. *To grant, concede*
[akin to Gr. δῐ'-δω-μι].
Dŏlĕo, ŭi, ĭtum, 2. v. n. *To
grieve, sorrow, mourn.*
Dŏlor, ōris, [doleo, 'to
grieve']. *Grief, sorrow.*
Dŏmĭna, æ, f. *Lady, mistress.*
Dŏmus, i and ūs, f. *A dwelling, abode, house, home*
[δόμος].
Dō-num, ni, n. 1. *A gift,
present.*—2. *A gift,* or *of-
fering,* to the gods.
Dōs, dōtis, f. *A marriage
portion, dowry.*
Dulc-is, e, adj. *Sweet, delightful* [usually referred
to γλυκύς].
Dum, conj. [akin to diu].
*While, whilst, as long as,
until.*
Dŭo, æ, o, num. adj. plur.
Two. — As Subst. : *Two
persons* [δύο].
Dūrus, a, um, adj. *Hard,
firm, harsh, stern, difficult.*
Dyspăris, ĭdos, m. *Ill-fated
Paris.*

Edĭtus, a, um, *part. of ĕdo.*
Edo, dĭdi, dĭtum, 3. v. a.
[e—do, 'to give']. *To
give forth,* in pass. *to be
sprung or descended from.*
Edo, ēdĭdi, ēdĭtum, ĕre. *To
give forth, to declare.*
Ego, Gen. mĕi (plur. nos),
pers. pron. *I.*
En interj. *Lo! behold! see!*
Enim, conj. *For.*
Eo, īvi, *or* ĭi, ĭtum, īre, v.
n. : 1. *To go.*—2. Impers.
Pass. : itur, *It is gone* by
one ; *i. e. one,* etc., *goes ;*
[Gr. ἰέναι, 'to go'].
Epistŭla, æ, f. *A letter.*
Ergo, adv. [akin to vergo,
'to bend']. *Therefore.*
Erŭo, ŭi, ŭtum, 3. v. a. *To
cast forth, stir up, plough
up.*
Et, conj.: 1. *And, also, too,*
—2. *Even* [Gr. ἔτι].
Ex (ē), prep. gov. abl. *From,
away from. Of, out of.*
[ἐξ].
Ex-cĭpĭo, cēpi, ceptum, ĕre.
To take out, accept. [From
ex, and căpio.]
Ex-cŭtĭo, cussi, cussum, cŭt-
ĕre, 3. v. a. [for ex-quătio].
1. *To shake out* or *from,*
—2. *To shake off, drive
away.*
Exemplum, i, n. *An exam-
ple, a precedent.*
Exĕo, ĭi, ĭtum, 4. v. n. and
a. *To go out, or forth.*
Exsanguis-e, adj. [ex-san-

guis, 'blood']. *Bloodless, pale, wan.*

Exsto, are, v. a.   *To stand out, to be visible, appear.*

Externus, a, um, adj. [*exter,* 'outward']. *Foreign, strange.*

Exŭo, ŭi, ūtum, 3. v. a. *To draw off, put off.*

Făcĭes, ēi, f. [facio]. *Face, form, aspect.*

Făcĭo, fēci, factum, ĕre, 3. v. a. *To make, to give.* In pass.:fĭo,fĭĕri,factussum. *To be made, to become.*

Factum, ĭ. n. [facio]. *A work, deed.*

Făgĭnĕus, a, um, adj, [fāgus, 'a beech']. *Of beech, beechen.*

Fāgus, i, f. [φηγός]. *A beech tree.*

Fallo, fĕfelli, falsum, ĕre, 3. v. a.   *To deceive, conceal.* Pass. : fallor, falsus sum [σφλλω].

Falsus, a, um, *part.*[*of fallo*]. *False.*

Falx, falcis, f.   *A pruning hook.*

Fāma, æ, f.   *Fame, reputation, renown* [φήμη].

Fămŭla, æ, f.   *A maid-servant, handmaid.*

Fas, inaecl. n [fari, ' to speak']. *Divine law, right, proper, permitted.*

Fātĕor, fassus sum, ēri, 2. v. dep. [fari, φάω]. *To confess.*

Fātīgo, āvi, ātum, 1. v. a. *To weary.*

Fā-tum, ti, n. [f (a)-or, 'to speak']. 1. *Destiny, fate.* —2. Plur. : Personified : *The Fates;* the goddesses of destiny.

Faunus, i, m. [făvĕo, 'to favour']. *The tutelary deity of agriculture, cattle and shepherds.*

Fax, făcis, f.   *A torch, flame.*

Fecundus, a, um [feo, 'to produce']. *Fertile, abounding in, full of.*

Fēlix, lĭcis, adj. [fĕ-o, ' to produce']. *Happy, fortunate, prosperous.*

Fēmĭnĕus, a, um, adj. [fēmĭna. 'a woman']. *Of a woman, female.*

Fĕro, tŭli, lātum, ferre, v. irreg. : *To bear, carry, obtain, endure, it is said, they say* [akin to φέρω).

Ferreus, a, um, adj. [ferrum, 'iron']. *Of iron, cruel.*

Ferrum, i, n. *Iron, a sword.*

Fertur, pres. ind. pass. of fĕro = *is said.*

Fĕr-us, a, um, adj. : 1. Of a n i m a l s : *Wild.* — As Subst.: (a) fĕrus, i. m. *A wild animal;* (b) fĕr-a, æ, f. *A wild beast.*—2. *Cruel, fierce, savage* [akin to θήρ, in Æolic dialect φῆρ, 'a wild animal'].

Fĭd-es ĕi, f. [fĭd-o, ' to

trust']. *Trust, faith, belief.*
A given *promise, a pledge.*

Fīo, fīĕri. See facio.

Flam-ma, mæ, f. *A flame*
[fr. flag-ro, 'to burn or
blaze'; akin to Gr. φλέγ-
ω, 'to burn'].

Flāvĕo-ēre, v. n. [Flāvus,
'golden yellow']. *To be
golden yellow.*

Flēbĭlis, e, adj. [fleo, ' to
weep']. *To be wept over,
bewailed, lamented.*

Flĕo, flēvi, flētum, flēre, 2.
v. n. and a. *To weep, shed
tears, to weep for* [akin to
φλέ-ω, 'to gush or over-
flow'].

Fluc-tus, tūs, m [fr. flŭo, 'to
flow']. *A billow, wave.*

Flū-men, mĭnis, n. [flŭ-o,
' to flow']. *A stream, river.*

Flŭvĭālis, e, adj. [fluvius,
'a river']. *Of a river.*

Foedus-ĕris, n. [fido, 'to
trust']. *A league, covenant,
agreement, treaty, compact.*

Foenum, i, n. *Hay.*

Fŏlĭum, i, n. *A leaf.*

Fon-s, tis, m. [fr. fund-o,
'to pour forth']. *A spring,
fountain.*

Fŏr-is, is, f. *A door* [akin to
Gr. θύρ-α].

Formōsus, a, um, adj. [for-
ma, 'form']. *Finely formed, beautiful, handsome.*

Fortius, adv. compar. of for-
titer. *Bravely, valiantly.*

Frāter, tris, m. *A brother.*

Frētum, i, n. ['A strait'].
The sea.

Frons, dis, f. *A leaf.*

Fŭgax, ācis, adj. [fugio, 'to
flee']. *Prone to flee, fleeing.*

Fŭgĭo, fūgi, fŭgĭtum, fŭgēre,
3. v. n. *To flee.*

Fŭgĭtīvus, a, um, adj. [fugio,
'to flee']. *Fleeing away,
fugitive.*

Fulgĕo, fulsi, ēre, 2. v. n.
To flash, to shine.

Fū-mus, mi, m. *Smoke* [akin
to Gr. θι'-ω, 'to rush'].

Fū-nus, nĕris, n.: 1. *A dead
body, corpse.—2. Funeral
rites; a funeral, burial.—
3. Death.*

Fŭrĭōsus. a, um, adj. [furo].
Mad, raging.

Fŭro, ŭi, 3. v. n. *To rage
or be furious.*

Fŭror, ōris, m. [fŭro, 'to
rage']. *Rage, madness,
fury.*

Gălĕa, æ, f. *A helmet.*

Gaudĭum, ii, n. [gaudeo, 'to
rejoice']. *Joy, enjoyment,
pleasure.*

Gĕl-ĭdus, ĭda, ĭdum, adj.
[gĕl-o, ' to freeze']. 1.
*Freezing, frosty.—2. Cold,
icy cold.*

Gĕmellus, a, um, adj. dim.
[geminus, 'a twin']. *Twin
born.*

Gĕna, æ, f. *A cheek.*

Gĕnu, us, n. *A knee* [γόνυ].

Gĕn-us, ĕris, n. [gĕn-o, 'to bear or bring forth ']. A race, kind, sort.

Germūna, æ, f.   A sister.

Gĕro, gessi, gestum, gĕrĕre, 3. v. a. To carry on, conduct ; to carry, bear.

Grădus, ūs, m. [gradior]. A step, degree, rank.

Graius, a, um, adj. Greek, Grecian.

Grāmen, ĭnis, n. Grass.

Grandaevus, a, um, adj. [grandis, 'great,' aevum, 'age ']. In years, old, aged.

Grātus, a, um, adj. : 1. Delightful, dear, pleasing, agreeable. —2. Thankful, grateful. Comp.: grāt-ior [akin to χαρτ-ός, 'causing delight'].

Grăv-is, e, adj. 1. Heavy, weighty. — 2. Heavy, oppressive, grievous, hard, severe. Comp.: grăv-ior [akin to Gr. βαρύς].

Grĕmĭum, ii, n. The lap, bosom.

Grex, grĕgis, m. A flock, a herd.

Hăbĕ-o, ŭi, ĭtum, ēre, 2. v. a. To have, to hold, contain [prob. akin to ἅπτομαι].

Haemŏnis, ĭdis, f. A Thessalian woman.

Haemŏnĭus, a, um, adj. Of Haemonia (Thessaly).

Hærĕo, hæsi, hæsum, hær-ēre, 2. v. n. To hold fast, cling, belong.

Hasta, æ, f. A spear, javelin.

Hector, ŏris, m. The eldest son of Priam.

Hĕcŭba, æ, f. The daughter of Dymas, and wife of Priam.

Hei, interj. Ah! woe!

Hĕlĕna, æ, f. A daughter of Jupiter and Leda, and the wife of Menelāus.

Herb-a, æ, f. Sing. and Plur.: Pasturage, herbage, grass, food [akin to Gr. φέρβ-ω, 'to feed '].

Heu, interj. Alas!

Hic, hæc, hoc. (Gen. hūjus; Dat. huic), pron. dem. This.

Hĭems, ĕmis, f. [χειμων]. Winter.

H-in-c, adv. 1. From this place.—2. From this cause, hence. — 3. After this. Hinc atque hinc = on this side and on that.

Hos-pes, pĭtis, m. 1. A visitor, guest.—2. An entertainer; a host.—3. = Gr. ξένος: A guest-friend.

Hos-tis, tis, comm. gen. 1. A stranger or foreigner. 2. (a) A public enemy, a foe. (b) Plur.: The enemy, in collective force.

Huc. Hither.

Hūmĕo, ēre, v. n. To be moist, damp, wet.

Hŭm-ĭlis, ĭle, adj. [hŭm-us,

'the ground']. *Low, near the ground, mean.*

Hŭm-us, i, f. 1. *The ground.* —2. Opp. to æquor, 'sea,' *The land* [akin to χαμ-αί, 'on the ground'].

Ide, ēs, and Ida, æ, f. *A high mountain in Phrygia, near Troy.*

Ignis, is, m. *Fire.*

Il-le, la, lud (Gen. illīus; Dat. illi), pron. adj. [fr. is]. *He, she, it, they.*

Illic, adv. [illic (pron.), 'that']. *In that place, there.*

Illuc, adv. [adverbial neut. of illic, 'that']. *To that side* or *place, thither.*

Iliăcus, a, um, adj. *Ilian, Trojan.*

Ilĭon, ii, n. *A poetical name for Troy* (Ilus, one of the kings of Troy).

Imāgo, ĭnis, f. [akin to similis]. *Image, form.*

Imĭtor, atus, 1. v. dep. *To imitate, represent.*

Im-mensus, mensa, mensum, adj. [fr. in, 'not;' mensus, 'measured']. 1. Of extent: *Vast, huge, immense.* —2. *Boundless, infinite, endless.*

Imperfectus, a, um, adj. [in not perfectus, 'finished'] *Unfinished.*

Impĕtus, ūs, m. *Force, impetus, impetuosity.*

Im-plĕo, plēvi, plētum, 2. v. a. *To fill up.*

Im-pōno, pŏsŭi, pŏsĭtum, pōnĕre, 3. v. a. [fr. in, pōno]. *To put, place, set,* or *lay upon.*

In, prep. gov. abl. and acc.: 1. With Abl.: (a) In. —(b) *On, upon.* —2. With Acc.: (a) *Into.* —(b) *On, upon.* —(c) *For.* —(d) *To, unto.* —[Gr. ἐν].

Inăchĭus, a, um, adj. *Argive* or *Grecian.*

Inăchus, i, m. ["Ιναχος]. *Inăchus,* son of Oceănus, father of Io, and first King of Argos. The river Inăchus in Argŏlis was called after him.

In-certus, certa, certum, adj. [in, 'not,' certus, 'sure']. *Not sure, uncertain, doubtful.*

Incīdo, cīdi, cīsum, 3. [in-caedo, 'to cut']. *To cut into, inscribe.*

Incīsus, a, um, *part. of incīdo.*

In-cumbo, cŭbŭi, cŭbĭtum, cumbĕre, 3. v. n. [in, obsol, cumbo, (=cŭbo). *To lie down, to lean.*

Indignor, ātus, 1. v. dep. *To be indignant at.*

Indigne, adv. [indignus, 'unworthy']. *Unworthily, undeservedly.*

In-dŭo, dŭi, dūtum, dŭĕre, 3. v. a.: 1. *To put on garments, etc.* Pass.: in-dŭor, dūtus sum, dŭi [ἐν-δύω].

In-ers, ertis, adj. [fr. in, ars]. *Sluggish, slow, inactive*, etc.

Infēlix, īcis. adj. *Unhappy, unfortunate.*

Infĕro, tŭli, illātum, ferre, v. a. *To bring into*, cum Dat.

Infestus, a, um, adj. *Hostile, inimical.*

Ingĕmo, ŭi, 3. v. a. and n. *To groan or sigh over.*

Inīquus, a, um, [in ; aequus, 'favourable']. *Unfavourable, adverse, injurious, hurtful.*

Insignis, e, adj. [in, 'upon,' signum, 'a mark']. *Remarkable, noted, distinguished.*

Inūtĭlis, e, adj. [in, ' not,' ūtĭlis, ' useful ']. *Useless.*

Invĭdĕo, vīdi, visum, 2. v. a. and n. [in ; video, *to see*]. *To envy.*

Invītus, a, um, adj. *Unwilling, against one's will.*

Iō, interj. *Oh! Ah!*

Iphiclus, i, m. A son of Phylacus and Cleomene of Phylace in Thessaly, one of the Argonauts, and a swift runner.

Ipse, ipsa, ipsum, pron. dem. (is, this, that). *Self, very, identical.* As personal pron.: *One's self, its own self.*

Irrīto, āvi, ātum, 1. v. a. [Irrĭo, 'to snarl']. *To exasperate, annoy.*

Irrŭo, rŭi, 3. v. a. *To rush upon, or into.*

Is, ĕa, ĭd (Gen. ējus ; Dat. ēi), pron. dem. *This or that* person or thing. —As Subst.: (a) ĭs, m. *He.*— (b) ĕa, f. *She*—(c) ĭd, n. sing.: *The thing just mentioned, that thing*—(d) ĕa, n. plur. *The things just mentioned, those things.*

Is-te, ta, tud (Gen. istīus ; Dat. isti), pron. dem.[is ; demonstr suffix te]. 1. *This*, or *that*, person or thing.—2. *Such as this*, etc.

I-ter, tĭnĕris, n. [ĕo, 'to go']. *A road, way, path, course, journey*, etc.

Jăc-ĕo, ŭi, ĭtum, ēre, 2. v. n. 1. *To lie, lie down.*—2. *To be despised.*

Jam, adv. 1. *At that time ; then.* — 2. *At this time ; now, soon.*

Jŭbĕo, jussi, jussum, jŭbēre, 2. v. a. *To order, command, bid.* — Pass. : jŭbĕor, jussus sum, jŭbēri.

Jŭgum, i. n. [jungo]. *A yoke* for oxen.

Jŭgum, i, n. [jungo, ' to join']. *A yoke, a mountain ridge, height.*

Junctus, a, um, P. perf. pass. of jungo.

Jungo, junxi, junctum, jun-gĕre, 3. v. a. 1. *To join, unite.*—2. *To yoke.*—3. Pass.: *To be joined to,* i. e. *to sit close beside.*—Pass. : jungor, junctus, sum, jungi [akin to Gr. ζυγ, root of ζει'γννυμι].

Jūno : ōnis, f. *Juno,* the daughter of Saturn, sister and wife of Jupiter.

Juppĭter, Gen. Jŏvis, m. *Jupiter;* a son of Saturn, and mythic king of the heathen celestial deities.

Jūro, āvi, ātum, 1. v. a. [jus, 'right']. *To swear.*

Jussi, perf. ind. of jŭbĕo.

Jus-tus, ta, tum, adj. [fr. jus, jur-is]. *Just, upright.*

Juvenca, æ, f. [juvenis, 'young']. *A heifer, girl.*

Jŭvĕn-is, is, adj. comm. gen. *Young, youthful.*—As Subst.: *A young person; a youth, young man.*

Jŭvo, jūvi, jūtum, are. 1. v. a. *To delight, to avail.*

Lăb-or, ōris, m. *Labour, toil* [akin to Gr. λαβ, root of λα(μ)β-ανω, 'to take'].

Lăbōro, āvi, ātum, 1. v. n. [lăbor, 'labour']. *To labour, toil, strive.*

Lăcaena, ae, f. adj. *Lacedaemonian, Spartan.*

Lăcertus, i, m. *The upper arm, the arm.*

Lăcrĭma, æ (old form dacri-ma), f. *A tear* [akin to Gr. δάκρυ].

Lacrĭmōsus, a, um, adj. [la-crĭma, 'a tear']. *Mournful, lamentable.*

Lædo, læsi, læsum, lædĕre, 3. v. a. *To hurt, injure, harm.*—Pass.: lædor, læ-sus, sum, lædi.

Laetĭtia, æ, f. [lætus, 'joyful']. *Joy, gladness.*

Lūna, æ, f. *Wool* [λῆνυς or λάχνη].

Languĭdus, a, um, adj. [lan-gueo, 'to be languid']. *Languid, faint, weary.*

Lāŏdămīa, æ, f. *A daughter of Acastus, and wife of Prōtĕsĭlāus.*

Lassus, a, um, adj. *Faint, languid, weary.*

Lăt-ĕo, ŭi, no sup., ēre, 2. v. n. *To lurk; to lie hid or concealed* [akin to λαθ, root of λα(ν)θ-άνω, 'to lie hid'].

Lectus, i, m. [lego, 'to gather']. *A couch, bed.*

Ledaeus, a, um, adj. *Of Leda.*

Lēgĭtĭmus, a, um, adj. [lex, 'law']. *Lawful, legal.*

Lĕgo, lēgi, lectum, lĕgĕre, 3. v. a. *To collect, gather together. To read.*—Pass.: lĕgor, lectus sum, lĕgi.

Lēnĭter, adv. [lēnis, 'soft']. *Softly, mildly, calmly.*

Lĕv-is, e, adj. *Light, slight,*

trifling, fickle [akin to Gr. ἐ-λαχύς].

Lex, lēgis, f. [=leg-s ; fr. lĕg-o, ' to read ']. *A law, statute, decree, ordinance.*

Licet, licuit and līcĭtum, est. 2. *It is allowable, one may.*

Lingua, æ, f. *The tongue.*

Lintĕum, i, n. [linteus, 'made of flax ']. *A sail.*

Lĭtĕra, æ, f. (Lĭno). *A letter.*

Lītus, ŏris, n. *The shore, coast, beach, strand.*

Longaevus, a, um, adj.[lon-gus, 'long;' aevum, 'age']. *Of great age, aged.*

Longe, adv. [longus, 'long ']. *Far off, far away.*

Lūgĕo, luxi, luctum, 2.v. a, *To bewail, lament, mourn for.*

Lux, lūcis, f. *Light, day.*

Lympha, æ, f. *A water nymph, water.*

Măcŭla, æ, f. *A spot, a mesh.*

Mădĕo, ui, 2. v. n. *To be moist or wet, to be imbued with, to melt.*

Mădĭdus, a, um, adj. [ma-deo]. *Wet, watery.*

Maestus, a, um, adv. *Sad, sorrowful.*

Măg-is, comp. adv. [root MAG. See mag-nus]. *More; in a greater or higher de-gree: magis quàm, more than.*

Magistra, æ, f. *A mistress, a teacher.*

Mag-nus, na, num, adj.: 1. *Great.*—2. *Mighty, power-ful.* —3. *Noble, famous.* Comp. : mājor ; Sup. : maxĭmus [root MAG, akin to Gr. μέγ-ας].

Mūlus, i, c. *An apple tree, mast.*

Măl-us, a, um, adj.—1. *Bad.* —2. *Unfortunate, adverse, calamitous.* —As Subst. : mălum, i. n. *An unfor-tunate thing,* etc.; *i. e. A misfortune, calamity,* etc. Comp. : pējor ; (Sup. : pessĭmus) [akin to Gr. μέλ-ας, 'black'].

Mandā-tum, ti, n. [mand-(a)-o, ' to enjoin ']. *A charge, instruction, com-mission, command.*

Mando, ūvi, ūtum, 1. v. a. [manus, ' the hand;' and do, 'I give']. *To commit, consign.*

Măn-ĕo, si, sum, ēre, 2. v. n. *To remain, continue* [μέν-ω].

Mă-nus, nūs, f. 1. *The hand.* —2. *A band, or company.*

Margo, ĭnis, c. *An edge, brink.*

Mărīta, æ, f. [mas, 'a male']. *A married woman, wife.*

Mărīt-us, i, m. [mărīt-us, 'married']. *A husband.*

Matrōna, æ, f. [mater, ' a mother']. *A wife, matron.*

Medeor, 2. v. dep. n. *To heal, cure.*

Mĕdĭcābĭlis, e, adj.[medeor, 'to cure']. *That can be healed, curable.*

Mĕmor, ŏris, adj. *Mindful, reminding.*

Mendax, ācis, adj.[mentior, 'to lie']. *False, deceptive.*

Mĕnĕlāus, i, m. A son of Atreus, brother of Agamemnon, and husband of Helen.

Mĕrĕo, ŭi, ĭtum, 2. v. a. *To earn, deserve.*

Mĭco, ŭi, 1. v. n. *To quiver, palpitate.*

Mĭlītĭa, æ, f. [miles, 'a soldier']. *Military service.*

Millēsĭmus, a, um, [mille, 'a thousand']. *Thousandth.*

Minerva, æ, f. A Roman goddess, identical with the Grecian Pallas Athene, the daughter of Jupiter, and the goddess of wisdom.

Mī-ror, rātus, sum, rāri, 1. v. dep. *To wonder, or marvel at.*

Miscĕo, miscŭi, mistum, *or* mixtum, miscēre, 2. v. a. 1. *To mix or mingle.*—2. *To join, unite.*—3. *To throw into confusion, to disturb.* Pass.: misceor, mistus *or* mixtus sum, miscēri [akin to Greek μισγ-ω, μιγ-νυμι].

Mĭs-er, ĕra, ĕrum, adj. [prob. akin to mær-ĕo, 'to be sad;' mæs-tus, 'sad']. *Wretched, miserable:*—me miserum, *wretched me!* or *woe is me!*

Mĭsĕrābĭlis, e, adj. [miseror, 'to pity']. *Mournful, sad.*

Mĭsĕrĕor, itus, 2. v. dep. [miser, 'wretched']. *To pity.*

Mitto, mīsi, missum, mittĕre, 3. v. a. *To send, send forth.*—Pass.: mittor, missus sum, mitti.

Mōbĭlis, e, [moveo, 'to move']. *Easily moved, changeable.*

Mŏdĭce, [modicus, 'moderate']. *Moderately.*

Mœn-ĭa, ĭum, n. plur. *Walls* of a city [akin to ά-μυν-ω 'to ward off'].

Moestus, a, um, adj. [moereo, 'to be sad']. *Sad, sorrowful.*

Mōles, is, f. *An immense, or vast, mass.*

Mon-s, tis, m. [fr. mĭn-ĕo, 'to project']. *A mountain.*

Monstro, āvi, ātum, 1. v. a. [moneo, 'to remind']. *To show, point out.*

Mŏra, æ, f. *Delay.*

Mordĕo, mŏmordi, morsum, 2. v. a. *To bite, eat away.*

Mŏr-ĭor, tŭus, sum, i, 3. v. dep. *To die.*

Mŏr-or, atus sum, ari, 1. v.
dep. [mŏr-a, 'delay']. *To
delay, tarry, linger.*

M-ōs, ōris, m. *Usage, habit,
custom, practice.*

Multo, adv. *Much, by much,
far.*

Mūnĭtor, ōris, m. [munio,
'to fortify']. *A fortifier,
builder.*

Mūrex, ĭcis, m. *The purple
fish, purple dye, purple.*

Mūto, āvi, ātum, 1. v. a.
[moveo, ' to move']. *To
change, alter.*

Mycēnaeus, a, um, adj. Of
or belonging to Mycenae,
Myce-naean (Mycēnae,
arum. A celebrated city
in Argolis, of which Aga-
memnon was king).

Nātīvus, a, um, adj. [nascor,
'to be born']. *That is
produced by nature, natu-
ral.*

Nauta, æ, m. *A sailor, sea-
man.*

Necto, nexŭi, nexum, 3. v.
a. *To bind, join, tie,
weave.*

Nĕfas, n. indecl. [ne, 'not:'
fas, 'divine law']. *Im-
piety, wickedness.*

Nĕgo, āvi, ātum, 1. v. a.
To say no, to deny, refuse.

Neptūnus, i, m. The my-
thic brother of Jove, and
god of the sea.

Nē-que (nec), conj. and adv.
nĕ, 'not;' quĕ, 'and'].

1. Conj.: *And not, nor.*
Adv.: *Not.*

Nērēis, ĭdos, f. [Nēreus, 'a
sea god'], A daughter of
Nereus, a Nereid or sea-
nymph.

Nē-scĭo, scīvi *or* scĭi, scītum.
scire, 4. v. a. [ne-scio].
Not to know.

Nĭmĭ-um, adv. [nĭmĭ-us.
'too much']. *Too much.
too.*

Nĭ-si, conj. [ne, 'not;' si.
'if']. 1. *Unless, except.—
2. Save, but, except.*

Nix, nĭvis, f. *Snow* [νίψ,
νιφός].

Nŏcĕo, ŭi, ĭtum, 2. v. n. *T..
hurt, harm, injure.*

Nō-men, mĭnis, n, [no-sco].
A name, appellation.

Nōn, adv. *Not.*

Non-dum, adv. [non, 'not:
dum, 'yet']. *Not yet.*

Nō-sco, vi, tum, scēre, 3. v.
a. 1. In present tense
and its derivatives: *To get
or obtain a knowledge ; to
become acquainted with.
come to know.—2.* In per-
fect tense and its derivatives : *To have become acquainted with ; to know*
[old form gnō-sco ; Gr.
γι-γνώ-σκω].

Nūdus, a, um, adj. *Naked.
bare, needy.*

Nupta, ae, f. [nubo, ' to
veil']. *A married woman,
bride, wife.*

Nuptus, a, um, P. perf. of nūbo.

Nurus, ūs, f. *A daughter-in-law.*

Nympha, æ, f.: 1. *A bride, wife.*—2. *A nymph.*

Obortus, a, um, part. from oborior.

Ob-ŏrior, ortus, 4. v. dep. [oborior, 'to arise']. *To arise, spring up.*

Obscēnus, a, um, adj. *Ill-omened, fatal.*

Ob-sisto, stĭti, stĭtum, 3. v. n. *To set before, to oppose.*

Obsum, fui, obesse v.n. *To be against, be prejudicial to; to hinder, hurt, injure.*

Ocellus, i, m. dim. [oculus, 'an eye']. *A little eye, eyelet.*

Occurro, curri, rarely cŭcurri, cursum, 3. v. n. *To go to meet, to meet.*

Oculus, ŭli. m. *An eye* [akin to Gr. ὄκ-ος.]

Offendo, di, sum, 3. v.a. *To thrust, or strike against.*

Offensus, a, um, part. from offendo.

Of-fic-ĭum, ĭi, n. *A voluntary service, kindness, duty.*

Oenōne, es. f. *A Phrygian nymph, the daughter of Cebren, beloved by Paris, but afterwards deserted by him.*

Oppŏsitus, a, um, Pa. *Opposing, standing opposite.*

Oro, āvi, ātum, 1. v. a. [Os, 'the mouth']. *To beg, entreat, beseech.*

Oscŭlum, i, n. dim. [Os, 'a mouth']. *A kiss.*

Paene, adv. *Nearly, almost.*

Pallens, ntis. *Wan, pale.*

Pampĭnĕus, a, um. adj. [pampĭnus, 'a vine leaf']. *Full of vine leaves, decked with vine leaves.*

Par, păris, adj. *Equal.*

Parco, peperci, parcĭtum, or parsum, ĕre, 3. v. a. Cum dat. *To spare.*

Păris, ĭdis, m. A son of Priam and Hecuba, who carried off Helen, and thus caused the Trojan war.

Părĭter, adv. [par, 'equal']. *Equally, jointly.*

Păr-o, āvĭ, ātum, āre, 1. v.a. : 1. *To prepare, make or get ready,* etc.—2. *To get, obtain, acquire* [prob. akin to Gr. φέρ-ω, Lat. fér-o].

Par-s, tis, f. 1. (a) *A part, portion.* — (b) Adverbial Abl. : parte, *In part, partly.* — 2. Of persons : *A part, some* [akin to φαρω, 'to cut'].

Par-vus, va, vum, adj.[prob. akin to par-s). 1. Pos. : *Small, little.*—2. Of persons : *Little, youthful, young.* Comp. minor ; Sup. : minĭmus.

Pasco, pāvi, pastum 3. v. a. To pasture, feed.

Pastor, ōris, m. [pasco, 'to feed']. A feeder, a shepherd.

Pecto, pexi, pexum, and pectilum, 3. v. a. To comb.

Pēgăsis, ĭdis. f. 1. Of Pegasus—2. A fountain nymph (πηγή).

Pělăgus, i. n. The sea.

Pellex-īcis, f. A concubine, rival.

Perlĕgo, lēgi, lectum, ĕre, 3. v. a. [per-lego]. To survey, scan, examine.

Permănĕo, mansi, mansum, 2. v. n. To continue, endure, remain.

Pertĭmesco, mŭi, 3. v inch. a. and n. To fear greatly.

Pēs, pĕdis, m. A foot [akin to Gr. πούς. ποδ-ός].

Pessĭmus, a, um. Sup. of mălus.

Pĕt-o, ĭvi or ĭi, ītum, ĕre, 3. v. a. To seek [akin to Gr. πίπτω, 'to fall' and πέτομαι, 'to fly.']

Phĕraeus, a, um. adj. Of Phĕrae, a city of Thessaly.

Phœbus, i. m. Phœbus; a poetical name of Apollo, the sun-god [Φοῖβος].

Phylăcēis, ĭdis, adj. f. Of Phylace.

Pĭ-us, a, um, adj. Devout, pious. Tender, affectionate, loving.

Pīnus, ūs and i, f. : 1. A pine-tree, fir-tree; a pine, fir.—2. As built of pine or fir : a ship, vessel.

Plang-o, planxi, planctum, plangĕre, 3, v. a. To strike, smite, beat [πλαγ, root of πλήσσω, 'to strike'].

Plōro, āvi, ātum, 1. v. a. Lament, bewail.

Pŏly-dămas, antis, m. A Trojan.

Pōpŭlus, i, f. A poplar tree.

Post-quam, adv. After that, when.

Pŏtens, ntis, (P. pres. of possum), adj. Powerful, mighty.

Præ-bĕo, bŭi, bĭtum, bēre, 2. v. a. [præ-hŭbĕo]. To give, grant, furnish, afford, offer.

Praeceps, cĭpĭtis, adj. [praecaput, 'the head']. Head-foremost, steep, rapid.

Praecinctus, a, um, part. from praecingo.

Praecingo, nxi, nctum, 3. v. a. To gird, encircle.

Prae-mŏnĕo, ŭi, ĭtum, 2. v. a. To forewarn, admonish.

Præpōno, ĕre, pŏsŭi, pŏsĭtum, 3. v. a. To place before, to add.

Præterĭtus, a, um, P. perf. pass. of prætereo. Past.

Priămīdes-ae (Priamus, last king of Troy). A son of Priam.

Prŭīna, æ, f. *Hoar frost, rime.*

Prō-cumbo, cŭbŭi, cŭbĭtum, 3. v. n. *To fall, sink.*

Prō-dūco, duxi, ductum, 3. v. a. *To lead forward, to prolong, extend.*

Profĭcĭo, fēci, fectum, 3. v. n. [pro-facio, 'to make ']. *To go forward, profit, avail, accomplish.*

Prŏfundum, i. *A depth, the deep, the sea.*

Prŏhĭbĕo, ui, ĭtum, 2. v. a. [pro-habeo, 'to hold']. *To hold back, hinder, forbid.*

Prō-mitto, mīsi, missum, mittĕre, 3. v. a. [pro-mitto]. *To promise.*

Promptior, adj. comp. of promptus, a, um. *Ready.*

Prŏpĕro, āvi, ātum, āre, 1. v. n. [properus]. *To hasten.*

Prŏpĭor, ius, ōris, adj.— [Comp. of obsol. propis]. *Nearer.* Superl. proximus.

Prōra, æ, f. (πρῷρα). *The prow of a ship.*

Prōsĕquor, sĕcūtus, 3. v. dep. *To follow.*

Prŏtervus, a, um, adj. [protero, 'to rub']. *Violent, rude, wanton, pert.*

Prōtĕsĭlāus, i, m. A son of Iphiclus, a native of Phylace, in Thessaly.

Prūdens, ntis. adj. (provident, foreseeing). *Wise, prudent.*

Pŭdendus, a, um, part. of pudeo. *Shameful.*

Pŭdĕo, ŭi, or pŭdĭtum est, ēre, v. a. *To be ashamed.*

Pudicitia, æ, f. [pudeo, 'to be ashamed']. *Chastity, modesty.*

Pŭella, æ, f. *A little girl, maiden.*

Pŭĕrīlis, e, adj. [puer, 'a child']. *Childish, youthful.*

Pugno, āvi, ātum, 1. v. n. [pugna, 'a battle']. *To fight, do battle.*

Puppis, is (Acc. and Abl. mostly puppim and puppi), f: 1. *The hinder part of a ship; the poop or stern.*—2. *A ship, vessel.*

Purpŭra, æ, f. [πορφυρα]. *Purple.*

Purpŭra, æ, f. *Purple, a purple garment.*

Purpŭrĕus, a, um, adj. [purpura, 'purple']. *Purple-coloured, purple.*

Pŭt-o, āvi, ātum, āre, 1. v. a. [put-us, 'clean, clear']. *To deem, hold, think, suppose.*

Quā, adv. 1. *In which place, where.* 2. Ne qua = *lest in any way.* 1. *In which place, where.* 2. *In what way or manner; how.*

Quando, adv. *When,* conj. *since.*

Quĕrēla, æ, f. [quĕror, 'to complain']. *Complaint, lamentation.*

Quĕror, questus, 3. v. dep. *To complain.*

Quĕrŭlus, a, um, adj. [quĕror, 'to complain']. *Complaining, mournful, plaintive.*

Quis-quis, quod-quod, *or* quid-quid, *or* quic-quid, pron. indef. *Whatever, whatsoever,* person *or* thing.—As Subst.: quisquis, m. *Whoever, whosoever.*

Quis-que, quæ-que, quodque, pron. indef. [quis, 'any;' suffix que]. *Each, every, any.* As Subst. : quisque, m. *Each one, each.*

Quōcumque. *Whithersoever.*

Quon-dam, adv [from quom, old form of quem; suffix dam]. 1. *Once, once upon a time, formerly.—2. At some time, at any time, sometimes.*

Quŏque, conj. *Also, too.*

Quŏ-t-ies, adv. [quot, 'how many']. *How many times; how often.—2. (a). As many times, as often.—(b) As many times as, as often as.*

Quŏtus, a, um, adj. [quot, 'how many']. *How many, which or what in order, number, etc.*

Rādix, īcis, f. [ρά δıξ). *A root].*

Răp-ĭdus, ĭda, ĭdum, adj. [răp-ĭo, 'to tear.' *etc.*] *Tearing or hurrying along, swift, rapid, etc.*

Răpĭo, ŭi, tum, 3. v. a. *To drag or hurry away, to carry off, seize.*

Raptus, a, um, part. of răpĭo.

Rătis, is, f. *A bark, vessel, ship,* [Gr. ἐρέσσω, 'to row;' ἐρετ-μόν, 'an oar;' Lat. remus, 'an oar '].

Rĕcens, utis, adj. *Recent, fresh.*

Rĕcŏlo, cŏlŭi, cultum, 3. v. a. *To till again, recall.*

Recta, adv. [rego, 'to keep straight']. *Straightway, right on.*

Recurro, curri, 3. v. n. *To run back.*

Rĕdux, ŭcis, adj. [rē, duco, 'to lead']. *That leads or brings back.*

Rĕfĭcĭo, fēci, fectum, 3. v. a. [re, facio, ' to make ']. *To make again, restore, revive.*

Rēgĭa, æ, f. [regius, 'royal']. *A regal abode, a palace.*

Rĕlūcĕo, luxi, 2. v. n. *To flash, shine brightly.*

Rĕmŏvĕo, ōvi, ōtum, 2. v. a. *To remove, put aside, take away.*

Rēmus, i, m. *An oar.*

Rĕpărābilis-e, adj. [rĕpăro, 'to get again']. *That may be regained*

Rĕpertor-ōris, m. [rĕpĕrĭo, 'to find']. *A discoverer, inventor.*

Rĕpĕto, tīvi, tītum, 3. v. a. *To bring back, renew, repeat.*

Rĕposco, ĕre, v. a. *To demand back.*

Requĭesco, ēvi, ētum, 3. v. n. *To rest, repose.*

Rĕsisto, stĭti, 3. v. n. *To stand back, withstand, oppose.*

Resolvo, solvi, sōlūtum, ĕre, 3. v. a. *To unbind, loosen.*

Rĕspĭcio, spexĭ, spectum, spĭcĕre, 3. v. a. [fr. re ; spĕcĭo]. *To look back at.*

Rēte, is, n. *A net.*

Rē-tĭnĕo, tĭnŭi, tentum, tĭnēre, 2. v. a. [for rĕ-tĕnĕo]. *To detain, restrain.* Pass. rĕ-tĭnĕor, tentus sum, tĭnēri.

Retro, adv. [re, 'back']. *Backwards, back again.*

Rĕverentĭa, æ, f. [revereor, 'to respect']. *Respect, regard.*

Rĕvertor, versus sum, verti. 3 v. dep. *To turn back, to return.*

Rĕvŏcā-men, mĭnis, n. [re-vŏc(a)-o, 'to call back']. *A calling back, a recall.*

Rĕvŏco, āvi, ātum, 1. v. a. *To call back, recall.*

Rĭd-ĕo, rīsi, rīsum, rĭdēre, 2. v. a *To laugh at, deride, ridicule.*

Rĭgĕo, ēre, v. n. (ῥιγέω. frigeo). *To be stiff, rigid.*

Rĭgĭdus, a, um, adj. [rĭgĕo]. *Rigid, firm.*

Rīpa, æ, f. *The bank of a river.*

Rŏg-o, āvi, ātum, āre, 1. v. a. *To ask, beg.* Pass. : rŏg-or, ātus sum, āri.

Rŭdĭmentum, i, n. [rŭdis, 'rough']. *A beginning.*

Rumpo, rūpi, ruptum, 3. v a. *To break, interrupt, put a stop to.*

Rŭo, rŭi, rŭtum, 3. v. n. *To fall, to rush.*

Sāltim, usually saltem, adv. (a contraction of salutim, from salvus). *At least, at all events.*

Saltus, us. m. *A forest-pasture, woodland, forest.*

Sălūs, ūtis, f. [salveo, 'to be well']. *Health, safety.*

Saucius, a, um, adj. *Wounded or hurt.*

Sanguĭnĕus, a, um, adj. [Sanguis, 'blood']. *Bloody, blood-stained.*

Săpĭo, ĭvi or ĭi, 3. v. n. *To have a taste, to be prudent or wise.*

Sătŭro, āvi, ātum, 1. v. a. [sătur, 'sated']. *To fill, to dye.*

Sătyrus, i. m. *A satyr, a*

sylvan deity, companion of Bacchus.

Sceptrum, i. n. = σκῆπτρον A *sceptre*.

Scī-lĭcet, adv. [contr. fr. scīre-lĭcet, 'it is permitted to know']. *In good truth, indeed, forsooth.*

Scrībo, scripsi, scriptum, 3. v. a. *To write, to describe, celebrate.*

Sĕco, cŭi, ctum, āre, 1. v. a. *To cut.*

Sĕcundo, are, v. a. [sequor, 'to follow']. *To adjust, to favor.*

Sĕcundus, a, um, adj. *Second, favourable.*

Sed, conj. *But, yet.*

Sĕm-el, adv. : 1. *Once, but once, once for all.* 2. *At once* [akin to ἅ̔μ-α].

Sēmen, ĭnis, n. [sero]. *Seed.*

Semper, adv. [akin to sem-el]. *Always, ever.*

Sĕn-ex, is adj. [sĕn-ĕo, 'to be old']. *Old, aged.* — As Subst. : *An old man ;* Comp. : sĕn-ĭor.

Sĕqu-or, ūtus sum, i. 3. v. dep. : 1. *To follow.*—2. *To pursue* [akin to Gr. ἕπομαι].

Servus, i, m. [sibilated from ἐρύω, 'to drag away']. *A slave, servant, serf.*

Sĭmŭlācrum, i, n. [Sĭmŭlo, 'to make like']. *An image.*

Sinister, tra, trum, adj. *On the left hand or side. unlucky, unfavourable.*

Sĭno, sīvi, sītum, 3. v. a. *To allow, permit, suffer.*

Sīnus, ūs, m. *A bending, bosom, lap, garment.*

Sŏcer, ĕri, m. *A father-in-law.*

Sŏcĭus, i, m. *A friend, ally, companion, comrade.*

Sollĭcĭtus, a, um, adj. [Sollus, 'whole'; cieo, 'to move']. *Agitated, disturbed, anxious.*

Spargo, sparsi, sparsum. spargĕre, 3. v. a. *To sprinkle, scatter.* Pass : spargor, sparsus sum, spargi.

Spectābĭlis-e, adj. [specto, 'to look at']. *Visible. notable.*

Spec-to, tāvi, tātum, tāre, 1. v. a. and n. intens. [spĕc-ĭo, 'to see']. 1. Act. : *To look at, or towards; to gaze at or upon.*—2. Neut. : *To look, gaze,* etc.

Spēs, spĕi, f. [fr. spēr-o]. *Hope, expectation.*

Spīro, āvi, ātum, āre, 1. v. n. *To breathe.*

Splendĭdus, a, um, adj. [splendeo, 'to shine']. *Brilliant, noble.*

Squālor, ōris, m. [squāleo. 'to be stiff']. *Stiffness, squalor.*

Strāmen, ĭnis, n. [sterno 3, 'to spread']. *Straw, litter.*

Strēnuus, a, um, adj. *Brisk, active, energetic, vigorous.*

Suādĕo, suāsi, suāsum, 2. v. a. *To advise, recommend.*

Sŭb, prep. gov. Abl. and Acc. 1. With Abl. *Under, beneath.*—2. With Acc.: *Under, beneath* [akin to Gr. ὑπ-ό].

Sŭbĕo, īvi, or ĭi, ĭtum, 4. v. n. *To go under, to occur, advance.*

Sŭbĭ-tus, ta, tum, adj. [sŭbĕo]. *Sudden, unexpected.*

Subsisto, stĭti, ĕre, 3. v. n. *To stop short.*

Succĭdŭus, a, um, adj. [sub, cado, 'to fall']. *Sinking, failing.*

Sūcŭs, i, m. [sūgo, 'to suck']. *Juice.*

Sŭpēr, adv. *Thereupon, besides.* [ὑπερ].

Sŭperstes, stĭtis, adj. [super-sto, 'to stand']. *Surviving, outliving.*

Surgo, rexi, rectum, 3. v. a. [subrego 'to lead straight'] *To rise, arise.*

Suscĭto, āvi, ātum, 1. v. a. [sub-cĭto, 'to rouse']. *To lift up, swell.*

Suspĭcor, ātus, 1, v. dep. a. [suspicio, 'to look up at']. *To mistrust, suspect, surmise.*

Taenărĭus, a, um, adj. *Of Taenarus, Taenarian.*

Tam-quam (tan-quam), adv. *So as, just as, as it were.*

Tango, tĕtĭgi, tactum, tangĕre, 3. v. a.: 1. *To touch.* —2. Of places: *To come, or go, to: to reach, arrive at.*

Tant-um, adv. [adverbial neut. of tant-us]. 1. *So much.*—2. *Only.*

Tant-us, a, um, adj. : *So much; so great* or *large.*

Tĕgo, texi, tectum, tĕgĕre, 3. v. a. *To cover.*—Pass. : tĕgor, tectus sum, tĕgi [akin to Gr. στέγ-ω].

Tellūs, ūris, f.: 1. *The earth-* as opp. to the sea.—2. *A land, country.*—3. *Tellus,* the earth as a goddess, also called Terra.

Tĕmĕro, āvi, atum, 1. v. a. [tĕmĕre, 'rashly']. *To violate, dishonour.*

Tem-pus, pŏris, n. 1. (a) *A portion of time; a time, season.*—(b) *Time* in general.—2. Plur.: *Festivals.*

Ten-do, tĕtendi, tensum, or tentum, tendĕre, 3. v. a. and n. *To stretch, stretch out, extend.* Pass.:tendor, sus sum, di [akin to τεί-νω].

Tĕnebrae, ārum, f. plur. *Darkness.*

Tĕnĕdos, i, f. *An island in the Aegean sea. Its distance from the coast of Troy was forty stadia, or* something under five miles.

Tĕn-ĕo, ŭi, tum, ēre, 2. v. a. [akin to ten-do]. *To hold, have, keep possession of.*

. Terra, æ, f. 1. The *earth,* 2. The goddess *Terra,* same as *Tellus.*

Terreo, ŭi, ĭtum, ēre, 2. v. a. *To frighten.*

Thălămus, i, m. *A chamber.*

Thēseus, ĕi and eos, m. A king of Athens, son of Aegeus and Aethra; husband of Ariadne and afterwards of Phaedra.

Thessălis, ĭdis, adj. f. Thessalian.

Tŏtĭes, num, adv. [tot, 'so many']. *So many times, so often.*

Trĕmo, ŭi, 3. v. n. and a. *To tremble.*

Trĕmor, ōris, m. [trĕmo, 'to tremble']. *A trembling.*

Tris-tis, te, adj. *Sad, sorrowful, morose, gloomy.*

Trōas-ădis or ădos, adj. fem. Trojan.

Trōja, æ, f. (Tros, one of the kings of Troy). A city of Phrygia.

Truncus, i, m. *The stem, stock, trunk of a tree.*

Tu, tŭi (plur. vos. vestrum or vestri), pers. pron. *Thou, you* [Gr. τυ, Doric form of σύ].

Tŭli, perf. ind. of fĕro.

Tum, adv.: 1. *At that time, then.*

Tŭmĕo, ēre, 2. v. n. *To swell*

Tun-c, adv. [tum-ce]. *At that time, then.*

Turba, æ, f. *A crowd, multitude* [Gr. τύρβη].

Turpis, e, adj. *Unsightly, shameful, base.*

Tūs, tūris, n. [θύος]. *Frankincense.* In plur. tura.

Tū-tus, ta, tum, adj. [tŭĕor, 'to protect']. *Safe.* Comp.: tūtĭor; Sup., tūtissĭmus.

Tŭ-us, a, um, pron. poss. [tū, tŭ-ĭ]. *Thy, thine, your.* — As Subst. : tūi, ōrum, m. plur. *Those belonging to thee; thy friends.*

Tyndăris, ĭdis, f. Daughter of Tyndărus.

Ulmus, i, f. *An elm tree, elm.*

Ultrix, ĭcis, adj. [ulciseor, 'to avenge']. *Avenging, vengeful.*

Ulŭlātŭs-ūs, m. [ululo, 'to howl']. *Wailing, shrieking.*

Unguis, is, m. *A nail of the finger.*

Usque, adv. *Continually.*

Vacca, æ, f. *A cow.*

Văle or vălĕas, in leave-taking. *Farewell, adieu.*

Vălĕo, ŭi, ĭtum, 2. v. n. *To be strong.*

Vātes, is, comm. *A prophet, a poet.*

Vātĭcĭnor-ātus, 1. v. dep. n. and a. [vates, 'a prophet']. *To foretell, prophesy.*

Vĕho, vexi, vectum, vehere, 3. v. a. *To carry, convey.*

Vel, conj. [akin to vŏl-o]. *Or if you will; or:*—vel . . . vel, *either . . . or.*

Vēlo, āvi, ātum, 1. v. a. [vēlum, 'a covering']. *To cover, wrap, envelope.*

Vē-lum, li, n. [fr. vĕh-o, 'to carry']. *A sail.*

Vēnātus, us, m. [vēnor I, 'to hunt']. *Hunting, the chase.*

Vĕnĭo, vēni, ventum, vĕnīre, 4. v. n. *To come.*

Vent-us, i, m. *The wind.*

Vĕnus, Vĕnĕris, f. The goddess of love, mother of Æneas. Veneris mensis = April, as if from Aphrodīte, her Gr. name.

Verbum, i, n. *A word.*

Vēro, adv. [vērus, 'true']. *In truth, assuredly, indeed.*

Verso, āvi, ātum, 1. v. a. intens. [verto, 'to turn']. *To turn often, upturn.*

Verto, verti, versum, vertĕre, 3. v. a.: 1. *To turn.*

—2. *To alter, change.*— Pass.: vertor, versus sum, verti.

Vēr-us, a, um, adj. *True.*

Ves-ter, tra, trum, pron. poss. [for vos-ter; fr. vos]. *Your.*

Vincĭo, vinxi, vinctum, 4. v. a. *To bind.*

Virgo, ĭnis, f. *A maiden, virgin, girl.*

Vĭrĭdis, e, adj. [vireo, 'to be green']. *Green.*

Vītis, is, f. *A vine.*

Vīto, āvi, ātum, 1. v. a. *To avoid, shun, escape, evade.*

Vīvo, vixi, victum, vīvere, 3. v. n. *To live.*

Vix, adv. *Scarcely, with difficulty.*

Vŏlo, āvi, ātum, 1. v. n. *To fly, speed, hasten.*

Vŏl-o, vŏlŭi, velle, v. irreg. With inf.: *To wish,* or *desire, to do,* etc. [akin to Gr. Βούλομαι].

Vō-tum, ti, n. [fr. vŏv-ĕo, 'to vow']. *A vow.*

Vuln-us, ĕris, n. *A wound.*

Vul-tus, tus, m. [prob. vol-o, 'to wish']. *Expression of countenance, mien, looks, countenance.*

Xanthus-i, m. *A river of Troas.*